The Curious Tale of the Homeless Man

A NOVEL

MONDE NKASAWE

ISBN: 978-1-77605-634-7
eISBN: 978-1-77605-633-0

Editing: Anine Vorster

Typesetting: Janet Von Kleist
jvonkleist@yahoo.com

Published by Kwarts Publishers 2020
www.kwartspublishers.co.za

DEDICATION

To my family, and to my readers: I'm humbled beyond words by your support of my writing, and by the positive feedback you have given to me since I started writing. A special word of thanks goes to my friends Nqabakazi Tetyana, Neliswa Maceba and Nomfanelo Kota who took the trouble to review and spot typos in the manuscript. As they say in my language: "*Ukwanda kwaliwa ngumthakathi.*"

Contents

ABOUT THE AUTHOR

Monde Nkasawe is a prolific writer, who has within a short period of five years written a poetry anthology and seven novels, all of which were published by Kwarts Publishers as well as Sifiso Publishers, namely:

1. Journey of the Heart
2. The Death of Nowongile
3. Pieces
4. Liziwe
5. The Madness of Rodney Makhelwane
6. The Fullness of Time
7. Go to the Eastern Cape

   (All published by Kwarts Publishers) and

8. We Need a Country (Published by Sifiso Publishers)

Victory

And then we bask in victory!
That which we celebrate with unrestrained passion.
Revelling and carousing with gay abandon.
Yelling: We won! We won! We won!
When in truth merely all we did was to effect the enemy's retreat,
Not his elusive demise.

Like a mouse that sees cheese,
Gleefully leaving its safe hole,
For the comfortable dangerous living room.
Seeing, smelling and hearing nothing else but the cheese
But fails to see the snake that hisses in the dark

We bask in this thing,
This juvenile, intoxicating thing!
Boastfully beating our chests,
Blissfully unaware of a simple fact,
But which the enemy is studiously alive to:
That staying in victory is more than fighting for it.
As it is perversely enjoyed by the losers too.
As, in truth, it curtails not only the loser's,
But victor's freedom too!

Willingly we ignore the mind's whispered warnings,
That those who offer us the bounty, have malice.
That quite like poisoned cheese,
The cup that overflows with spoils,
Is too a poisoned chalice.

But alas, the grumbling stomach,
Dulling all our senses.
Dulling us to any sense that to win, is too to lose,
The freedom not to care.
As freedom tastes sweet in pursuit,
But ends when gained.

PROLOGUE

"Yebethuna nal' igeza lisenz' umhlol' engcwabeni!" the mourners murmured in suppressed excitement. With absolute fascination, they watched "the Madman of Zwide Cemetery", as they called him, as he seemed to want to replace the clergy near the grave. It was the strangest thing, and as they gasped in utter shock, they whispered their bewilderment in a string of unanswered questions: What was going on? Who was he? What did he want? Was he even aware he was disrupting a sombre funeral? Did he lose something? Did he want to do the liturgy himself perhaps?

But for all he cared – this homeless man, who also went by the name of John – the mourners and their questions were as good as not even there. Standing over that grave, looking like he'd lost something inside the grave and was desperate for it not to be buried with the coffin, the man was as frightening a sight as he was fascinating.

Tall and well built, he wore a shirt which had clearly changed colour from being white to shiny black. Its sleeves were torn, revealing well-developed biceps. His face was rotund, glazy and with a deep dark pigmentation. His hair was long, reaching over his shoulders, and it looked like it had long won the battle with the comb. His dishevelled look was complemented by the battered jeans he was wearing, and the fact that he was barefoot.

As he stood near the grave, he seemed in absolute amazement as the singing among the mourners intensified. When he saw the coffin being placed on the lowering device, just before it would be winched down, his eyes seemed to pop out of their sockets, and as the congregation went into overdrive, singing 'Hamba naye Msindisi' to the accompaniment of a cacophony of makeshift instruments, including whistles, school handbells, drums, and bullhorns, he seemed just about ready to eat his head!

John watched with a growling look at the mourners as they danced in unison, as if they were one giant paste, uniformly bobbing sideways, with some of them regularly punching the air and yelling "kuyahanjwa!" To those observing him among the mourners, he seemed utterly displeased that the priests were allowing this funeral to continue, and at times it seemed like it's only the hand of God restraining him from lunging onto the lead priest.

Now convinced that the madman's dramatic presence was a sign from God that the deceased left before his time, the mourners observed him with increased intensity. They saw his entire body seeming to reflect the tension of a boxing spectator. They observed as he moved even closer to the gravesite, further heightening the dramatic moment.

What of course nobody knew was that even though ordinarily John would keep away from a funeral ceremony, as he believed there was nothing new to be seen, today he was puzzled as to why the mourners did not see what he thought they would see in the grave. Like a child who had seen a stranger peeking through a window, but was not there anymore, he knew there was something at this grave, and that they were mad for not seeing it!

Again, he came closer, almost alongside the last rites priest standing right on top of the grave, and his astonishment grew as he realised that the grave looked as normal as it should! He swore under his breath, *"Umhlola wamagqwirh' aseZwide!"*

Among the crowd who were observing John's curious behaviour were two cemetery security guards, Ntanjana and Jongile. When the strange funeral was over, these two guards left for the nearby township of Zwide, which was located on the outskirts of the Eastern Cape metropolis of Port Elizabeth. Uppermost in their minds was nothing more than to get hammered and forget about the witchcraft in their workplace!

Their day shift was over. But they could not go home yet, because the guys working the night shift had disappeared, and their phones were off. Their management back at the office had decided that these two guards must also go on and work the night shift, without a break, until a proper plan is made.

At about seven o'clock in the evening, Ntanjana and Jongile returned to the cemetery to complete their double duty, albeit reluctantly. *"Broer,* I'm not in the mood for all this nonsense today!" Ntanjana said, looking grumpily at his friend.

"What do you mean?" Jongile asked, exaggeratedly puzzled.

"I mean this, this coming to work twice in one day!" Ntanjana replied.

"I see, well it doesn't matter now, does it? We are here. I say, let's make the most of it. It's good money. Besides, we agreed to do this," Jongile said.

"Fine. But agreement or no agreement, I say let the damn ghosts take care of themselves for once. I am not doing any goddamn patrolling today. Management must sort out its own issues because I didn't sign up for slavery. I say, let's go to the guardhouse and drink!" Ntanjana said, with a rather drunken shrill tone of voice.

Of course, what Ntanjana was saying was no departure from the norm anyway. To both of them, being on duty always meant that they would sit at the guardhouse and talk about everything under the sun (or the moon as the case may be) while working their way through copious amounts of liquor bought at nearby taverns. They would never really do any 'security' work, such as patrolling around the cemetery. Even though they had agreed to the overtime arrangement of working both during the day and at night, they had no intention of actually fulfilling this. To them, working at night meant nothing more than being merely present at the place of work at night.

Today their attitude to work was particularly bad. At just after seven in the evening, two hours after they were supposed to report for duty, the two drunken security guards staggered and stumbled their way into the guardhouse of the Zwide Cemetery. The place was eerily deserted, which was a sharp contrast to earlier in the day when throngs of mourners had gathered at every part of the cemetery.

At the guardhouse, they found John, the homeless man, standing by the door waiting for them. In typical drunken alacrity, as soon as they saw him, the two guards both assailed John with demands that he should tell them a story.

"*Yizanazo Jambase! Balisa mfondini ubusuku buyahamba!*" Ntanjana said, yelling at the top of his voice, and throwing himself on the battered couch, which was the only furniture item in the guardhouse, and whose springs had taken much similar abuse for too long.

"*Ewe Hlathi mfondini*, your behaviour today was very strange, to say the least. *Yintoni mfondini ukusoyikisa kangaka, ubutyiwa yintoni*? asked Jongile, with an overpitched emphasis, waving a half-empty beer bottle about, and also staggering towards the same couch.

John, the homeless man, had over the years made a habit of treating the guardhouse of the Zwide Cemetery as his home. He would go anywhere around the Zwide township and would sometimes go away for days on end. But he would always return to the cemetery guardhouse. Both Ntanjana and Jongile, as well as many other guards with whom they changed shifts at the cemetery, were familiar with him.

In fact, they loved having him around, especially at night when he would regale them with stories. They loved him, not only because he could cover for them each time they went AWOL from night duties, but because he was such a great storyteller. They did not mind his exaggerations and embellishments. They loved that he could tell a story about what happened in Johannesburg, Cape Town, Durban, or even New York, even though they knew he had never been to any of those cities.

Everybody just referred to him as John. No one had any idea of what his real name was or where he was born. Those who were seeing him for the first time naturally assumed he was mad. The truth, though, was that no one knew anything about John, and none of his stories were actually about himself.

When he was not sitting in the guardhouse, his other spot was near the gate of the Zwide Cemetery. This spot was as inconspicuous as it was strange for anyone to want to live near the dead. Perhaps it was because of the phobia most people have about cemeteries, but over the years he'd been living in this place he found that very few of his homeless peers wanted to disturb him. He slept peacefully at night without anybody wanting to take his spot or steal from him.

What very few people knew, of course, was that John had found many years ago that mourners tended to be always in a generous and giving mood. Now at the age of 55, he had seen it all.

The Zwide Cemetery, situated along the R75, not far from Dora Nginza Hospital, was always busy on weekends, with an average of up to fifty funerals taking place in a weekend. From each funeral procession that entered the gravesite, John would make a killing as people somehow took pity on him begging not far from open graves.

As if to maximise the potential of this gig, he also helped around. Most of the time, he would look after the parked cars from a distance. But on occasion he would come closer to the actual funeral and would always be ready with a glass of water, taken from nearby taps, to offer an inconsolable mourner. Sometimes the gravediggers would make wrong measurements as a result of which the coffin would be stuck. John would always be ready to calm the panicking and embarrassed mourners about how such things always happen.

There were even worse instances of something very wrong happening. One time the lowering device that holds a coffin as it goes down snapped, sending the hapless coffin tumbling down! John was on hand to offer counselling.

On another day, burial societies were fighting about who had the rights to bury the deceased, with the losing one unceremoniously taking the deceased out of their coffin! Again, John was there to offer a steady hand of comfort to the acutely embarrassed mourners.

John also made it his business to clean the cemetery, especially on Fridays in anticipation of the weekend funeral services. In fact, the mayor of the Nelson Mandela Metro always had John topping the list of people to give Christmas presents to, each December.

Today the security guards were noticing that, as he was about to answer their questions about today's incident, John's demeanour had changed, from the jovial to deathly sombre. Unlike his usual boisterous manner of retelling a story, today he started with a whisper as if worried about someone listening to him.

Still, they wanted John to talk. Having settled into their usual come-and-drink routine, and had started to open a cheap bottle of brandy and beer cans, Ntanjana and Jongile wanted him to answer a few pointed questions about that incident which happened earlier during one of the many funerals which had taken place that day. In their drunken stupor, they wanted to know from John what was up with him.

It was cold. At just after eight in the evening, were it not for the lights that were on in most of the houses at Zwide Township, the whole place would be in pitch darkness. All the street lights were off, no doubt no longer functioning.

It being a Wednesday, the place was quiet. Unlike the Motherwell Cemetery on the other side of town, which was always bustling with mourners throughout the week, the Zwide Cemetery tended to be quieter on weekdays.

"Ok, ok guys, but we need stronger fire here. I'm a bit cold," John said, settling into his own usual comfortable routine of storytelling, which included rubbing his face as if he was waking up, and pulling his long and unkempt beard.

"First," John continued, "where are the guys who were on duty here last night? I too have questions to ask them."

Both Ntanjana and Jongile looked at each other as if struck by a sobering thought, and then Jongile said, "*Eish mfowethu, babhodile*! We don't know how. Management just told us they were found dead somewhere along the N2 towards Grahamstown, and that we should take their place on duty tonight."

"*Jonga Hlathi mfondini*, stop depressing us, just tell us your story, man!" Ntanjana interjected drunkenly.

Of course, what both Ntanjana and Jongile did not know was that what John was about to tell them was a story that made him to be deeply worried about his own state of mental health, and the news of the death of last night's shift did not help matters. He had definitely seen close to ten young white men alighting from a big truck, briefly saying something to the security guys, and then going back to the truck. He had seen them coming out the truck carrying what definitely looked like coffins, and he counted eight of them. He had seen the young white men putting the coffins inside freshly dug graves that were ready for the following day's funerals. He did not see what they did at the graves but had seen them huddling in the same way that mortuary people do when they put a coffin inside a grave. He knew that the graves belonged to families, some of whom he knew, and he had also seen the graves register at the guardhouse.

John remembered that when he saw the truck offloading the coffins at night and placing them inside the dug graves, his first thought had been that the families were doing advance burial of some kind, linked to whatever family ritual prevailed, strange as that sounded. But when the funeral processions came the following day, with coffins on tow, John's puzzlement grew exponentially, especially as none of the families were noticing that the graves they were using were already occupied!

Settled and ready to start telling the story, he looked at both Ntanjana and Jongile, and said, "Well, gentlemen, since you insist, let's go back to the beginning. It was the winter of July 1989, somewhere in the Transvaal ..."

SOMETIME IN
1989

The Betrayal of the Volk

"This is Radio South Africa. The time is one o'clock. The news is read by John Inglewood. In news just in, in a brief statement to the media, the office of the President has confirmed that this morning, President PW Botha met with the leader of the banned African National Congress, Mr Nelson Mandela, who is currently serving a life sentence at Pollsmoor Prison in Cape Town. The meeting took place at Tuynhuis in Cape Town. Details are sketchy at the moment, but Radio South Africa promises to provide these in later bulletins ..."

It was the 5th of July 1989, a day of sharp contrasts, from extreme excitement to deranged panic, accompanied by muted mutterings of betrayal. Every news outlet in the world was running with the story of the secret meeting between the jailed Nelson Mandela and the leader of the apartheid government, President PW Botha.

The excitement among activists was palpable. In gatherings that took place that day in stadiums, community halls, in churches and in the street, it was clear the meeting was being interpreted as the beginning of the fall of the apartheid regime, and it further galvanised mass commitment – that the struggle continues, *aluta continua! Certa Victoria!*

There were, of course, those among the selfsame activists, to whom it seemed strange that amid the conflagration characterised by ever-intensifying street battles in all the townships, and wars in most of the southern African region, there would be someone talking peace before the goals of all this warring have been attained. To be sure, they were a minority, and their voices of dissent were quickly swept away by the tide of excitement at the prospect of a very near *uhuru*.

But the news was also met with extreme anger among huge sectors of the white population, especially the far right wing. Following the Mandela/Botha meeting, the question of what is to be done was asked with similar urgency by those excited by the likely outcomes of this meeting, and those absolutely horrified by those outcomes. As the ANC began talking to its members about negotiations being a site of struggle, where it would demand the establishment of a constituent assembly to draw up a new constitution, in which one man, one vote would be the key provision, a significant sector of the white society began to ponder the question differently.

A day after the news of the meeting broke, with Afrikaans newspapers showing, as if mocking, pictures of a beaming Mandela in the company of the President, the Minister of Justice and the head of the intelligence service, a retired Major General Jan Kloppers, called two fellow former soldiers to his farm just outside the town of Schweizer-Reneke, ostensibly to have a braai. But this was, in fact, an urgently convened meeting intended to plot the reaction of the white community to the betrayal represented by the Mandela/Botha meeting. Present in the meeting were SADF's military veterans, Lieutenant Colonel Hein Terblanche, and Lieutenant Colonel Andy Malan.

The meeting was brief and to the point. Standing in a huddle outside the farmhouse near a fireplace, and all three of them holding Castle Lager beer cans, Lieutenant Colonel Hein Terblanche started by saying, "General Kloppers, command us, as you did in South West. Our people cannot be betrayed like this."

"What PW is doing cannot be allowed to stand. *Ek stem ook saam*, command us, General," Colonel Malan concurred.

"Well, Gentlemen, no disagreement here," said General Kloppers, and continued, "the situation calls for the *volk* to take action to preserve itself. But as we do so, we have to be very careful, lest we take premature action and be quashed immediately and permanently afterwards."

"Still, General, we cannot sit and do nothing!" Lieutenant Colonel Terblanche said pleadingly.

"I'm not saying let's do nothing. I'm saying let's be careful. I have a plan whose execution I want you to drive. You see, I'm a retired army general. That means I'm under watch for any potential mischief I may get myself into. It would not take long before it is not known that I'm involved. This means we must not take precipitative action. We must make a quiet, and long-term plan," General Kloppers said.

"A long-term plan, General?" Lieutenant Colonel Terblanche asked.

"You see, when I worked in the Transkei a few years ago, assisting the Transkei Defence Force to improve their training methods, one of the things I learned is this Xhosa saying, '*induku ibekwe emgqubeni*.'"

"What does that mean?" Colonel Terblanche asked.

"I may not be saying this right, of course, but it means literally that if you hide a stick underground, not only is it available for you to use in the future but in the time it lies underground it gains in strength. The plan I have in mind is modelled on the essence of the meaning of this phrase," General Kloppers said.

"Right. But what is that plan?" Colonel Malan asked.

"It's simple actually, and it is premised on us accepting that even though we did not lose the shooting war, the strength of the enemy is currently such that we cannot continue to shoot at it without doing untold damage to our people. That means whatever is going to happen after this betrayal meeting, let it happen."

"What do you suggest we do then General?" Lieutenant Colonel Terblanche asked bewildered.

"Well, hear me out, will you? Let the voice of our people echo through time. We have the means of eviscerating the enemy, with just one strike. Firstly, we have resources at Pelindaba. Before they close it, let's lift some of the material and develop it on our own, using the capacity of our people. As you know, for now, it is our people who work in that establishment, and they are unhappy. Let us tap on that unhappiness. Secondly, let us establish people's armouries across the country, ready to arm our people at a moment's notice. I'm quite sure there are people in the army willing to help us to build and supply arms caches throughout the country before our army is dissolved and taken over by the ANC army. Thirdly, I suggest that we also spend an initial amount of time collecting resources that will sustain this plan going forward. We have huge resources inside the Reserve Bank, and we can get a lot of that gold in no time," General Kloppers said as if he had been thinking about this for some time.

There was silence, with the two former soldiers clearly weighing the pros and cons of what General Kloppers had just said. Lieutenant Colonel Hein Terblanche was to the first to break the silence, saying, "Do you think we should align in some way with the AWB?"

With his eyes popped out, General Kloppers shot back, "Definitely not! Those hot-headed louts are actually dangerous to the interests of white people. Their idea of self-determination is a return to the days of Verwoerd, to full-on apartheid, and to the return of Afrikaner republics. That is as impossible as this other stupid idea of a *volkstaat*. In their heads, there are no black people in South Africa, but a bunch of monkeys that must just be corralled to the zoo. We have done all this. That's why there are homelands. None of it has worked. Any effective defence of the white folk must be completely devoid of hatred of black people. Remember, the Afrikaner has the exact same problem the ANC identified in its strategy and tactics – what it refers to as colonialization of a special type. The country is physically integrated, and Afrikaners are in every corner of the country. Unlike the Israeli/Palestine situation, there can be no two-state solution here. As I see it, our strategic task is to ensure that black people govern, but with our consent and in our interests. That means we must go out of our way to cultivate amenable black leadership. That is why I spoke earlier about this being a long-term plan."

"I like it already. How do we proceed?" Colonel Malan said.

"Well, taking all the things I've just said into account, I suggest that you, Lieutenant Colonel Terblanche, you must do further work to elaborate and to concretise everything. I want you to work with Dr Han Erasmus. He's game. I'll have a chat with him again later today. I want him to be the brains behind the project. He has a better view of both the National Party's treacherous mind and our security forces' eager ears."

General Kloppers paused, looked at Lieutenant Colonel Any Malan, and said, "I have already identified seventeen black guys whom we must nurture and guide their growth within the ANC. You, Colonel Malan, your job is to babysit these guys. I'll give you their names. See to it that they never change their minds. Every year, till the project's maturity, we will deposit monies into their accounts to keep them interested and their mouths shut. What we want is to see them contesting every ANC election that takes them to the next highest office. I know some of them are not yet political at this point. As the ANC is being unbanned it is going to want to establish a legal presence in the country. That means it is going to establish structures at all levels of society. Your task is to follow this process closely and see to it that our guys are available to contest elections at every level, till they reach the NEC stage. In the next ten years, these guys must reach national profile status. We're placing you in charge of a fighting kitty for this purpose. Buy conference delegates, twist arms and do absolutely everything that supports the progress of these guys. If there is anyone more popular than our guys, we must take that person out, by any means necessary. If anyone among our guys shows any signs of changing their minds, act quickly and decisively."

Again, General Kloppers paused, and then said, "I, on the other hand, in order to safeguard the project, I will withdraw from any active involvement."

"I agree, General. I'll do as you suggest General. Shall we call this Project Echo, perhaps?" Lieutenant Colonel Terblanche asked.

"Alright, Project Echo it is," General Kloppers said, and continued, changing the subject "Anyway gentlemen, am I the only who thinks Naas Botha should hang up the boots now?"

The heated disagreement that followed this question put an end to all the conspiratory discussion they were having up to that point!

The Meeting of Numbers

It was Friday the 5th of January 1990, at just after nine o'clock in the morning. Signs of the New Year revelry were still visible all over the city. Christmas decorations were still hanging on street poles and walls of shopping malls, and Christmas lights were still decorating all the major streets in town. There was litter lying about in most streets, mostly empty beer bottles.

Pretoria was, of course, one of those cities which tended to empty out during the December holidays, along with Johannesburg and most places in Transvaal, with everybody rushing for the coast and rural areas in the hinterland. Still, the city did have its fair share of tourists, especially the nervous shoppers who relish the freedom to shop in less congested malls and to drive in less traffic on the roads.

Dr Hans Erasmus, the 61-year-old Director-General of the NIS, observed this scene moments after landing at Jan Smuts Airport from a two-day trip to London. Ordinarily, he too would have gone to Hermanus for the holidays were it not for the pressures of work. Even today, as soon as he landed, he had insisted on going straight to his office in Pretoria. His grandchildren would have to wait for their presents. There were urgent matters of state to deal with first.

Along the way from the airport, Dr Erasmus listened to the news on the radio and soon regretted the idea. It was the same old mess he left a few days ago. The country was on lockdown as a result of a sustained campaign of mass action everywhere in the country. There were reports of street burning of tyres, marches in every major city, crippling work stay-aways, worker strikes, business boycotts, shootings by the police, more detentions, and just a general state of murder and mayhem.

People everywhere were demanding the release of Nelson Mandela, the release of all the Rivonia trialists, the release of detainees, the unbanning of the ANC and its alliance partners. Even though there were still no liberated zones in the country, Dr Erasmus reckoned that all the same, what the ANC had done successfully through this persistent mass action was to create a parallel authority. A huge part of the country was no longer governable by the National Party government. The situation, compounded by the international isolation of the government as well as by the biting effects of the sanctions campaign, was untenable! Something had to give.

When Dr Erasmus arrived at his office just before ten o'clock in the morning, he found the place deserted. Everybody was still on holiday, and Dr Erasmus was not impressed. "With the war raging inside and at our borders, how could we close our eyes off like that?" he fumed, talking to himself. He would call some of the section heads and give them a piece of his mind, just as soon as he'd taken care of other matters.

One such matter was giving the President feedback on a draft speech which he intended to use for his opening of Parliament on the 2nd of February 1990. The draft had been sent to all members of the Cabinet and to all the security arms, including the Chief of Defence, the National Commissioner of Police and the intelligence services. He had confirmed with his PA that his own copy was on his desk, which indeed it was.

His task, which the President had specifically asked of him, was obviously to make the corrections he deemed necessary on the speech itself. But more important, he had to get in touch with critical stakeholders, including Nelson Mandela at Victor Verster Prison, the ANC in Lusaka, as well as friendly governments across the world, especially the United States, Britain, Germany and Taiwan.

At about four o'clock that afternoon, Dr Erasmus finally completed the consultations on the President's draft speech. By and large, the content was accepted by all. The governments of the US and UK promised good returns if the President stuck to the current version of the speech, including a promise to lift sanctions against South Africa, and they also offered themselves the role of being peace guarantors for any process of negotiations with the communist aligned ANC. The ANC too indicated its agreement with the draft but insisted that it would accept nothing else other than majority rule under one man one vote, and Mandela himself echoed this sentiment.

When Dr Erasmus was done with the consultations, he sighed deeply, feeling the strain of not having slept after his trip, and he also felt defeated. The positive reaction to the President's draft speech, with the ANC sounding gloating and somewhat triumphant in its tone, was not helping his mood right now. Of course, as a senior civil servant, he subscribed to the code of serving the government of the day.

But all throughout his career in the civil service, that code had never meant anything else other than acceptance of change of government between the parties that served in the whites-only parliament. The possibility of serving a terrorist government of the ANC, which this draft speech was ultimately projecting, was something his education had not helped him to countenance.

He thought about sharing this speech with seventeen other people. But no sooner had he thought of this was he stuck on the best way of doing it without increasing the possibility of the speech being leaked. He decided against the idea and instead opted to call these people one by one and brief them on the essential elements of the speech.

Dr Erasmus was now left with the task of briefing the President. But before he could do that, he received a call on his landline. For reasons only he would know, he became nervous about this call. The landline number in his office was not listed, and there were very few people who knew what it was. Yet he knew who this caller was even before he could answer. Slowly he picked up, and the caller, clearly not expecting to talk to anybody else but Dr Hans Erasmus, said, in English:

"*Dogs are marching south. I repeat, dogs are marching south. The meeting is in Kimberley, at three am. Call when you get there.*"

The caller dropped the line without waiting for a response from Dr Erasmus. Immediately after this call, Dr Erasmus dropped everything and rushed to his car in the basement. When they saw him running down the stairs, his two bodyguards took that as a cue to hurry him to some place, and they also rushed into the car with him. Dr Erasmus held out his hand and said, "Sorry guys, this one is for me only. Go home, I'll need you on Sunday, OK?"

"Sure, Doc, and be careful out there, Doc. These ladies are not playing!" said one of the guards.

"What ladies are you talking about now, Konrad?" Dr Erasmus asked, mildly puzzled.

"You know boss," Konrad said, winking.

"*Ag Konrad, gaan huis toe man!* Go home!" Dr Erasmus said.

As he drove away, leaving his bemused guards behind, Dr Erasmus chuckled and muttered under his breath, "The bugger thinks I'm having an affair!"

At just after five o'clock that afternoon, Dr Erasmus arrived at his house and immediately started to prepare to leave for Kimberley. There was nothing much to prepare. With his wife not at home, all he did was to change from the clothes he had

had on since leaving London the day before and put on a fresh pair of jeans, a red t-shirt, and tekkies.

He wanted to drive himself, and he wanted to be alone. As risky as this was, the VIP security guys had become familiar with this routine. They didn't like it, but it was what the DG wanted, and there was nothing they could do about it. Amongst themselves, they joked about the DG's quiet sojourns into the unknown, imputing adulterous liaisons somewhere unseen. Nothing, of course, could be further from the truth.

At about half-past five that afternoon, Dr Erasmus left Pretoria and headed for Kimberley. He enjoyed driving at night. There was something about the sound of the car's engine in the dark that seemed to give him a high of sorts. The 6-litre v12 engine of a Bentley Arnage elaborated this feeling.

He figured he would be in Kimberley just before midnight. As it happened, helped by what could only be described as horrendous speeding, at half-past twelve midnight, Dr Erasmus, arrived in a sleepy Kimberley, a city in the northern part of the Cape Province and known as South Africa's home of diamonds.

But of course, Dr Erasmus was not here as a diamond merchant. He had more serious business in mind. As soon as he arrived in the town centre, he stopped at a garage, and after filling up his car, and using its ablution facilities, he went to a nearby telephone booth and made a call to someone. "I'm here, at the Total Garage. Come get me."

He dropped the line without waiting for a response. He knew there was no need for this. After that, he waited in his car for about five minutes, and then a black Mercedes-Benz E-Class emerged onto the garage's forecourt and flashed its lights towards his direction. Dr Erasmus acknowledged by starting his car, and then followed the Benz out of the garage, the two cars heading towards what appeared to be the town's outskirts.

About fifteen minutes later the two cars came to what looked like a smallholding in an area of town called Roodepan, and they followed one another through an open large metallic gate and then parked in front of a similarly large farmhouse. The time now was just after one o'clock in the morning. The place was quiet, with no indication of anyone or anything in it being alive.

Dr Erasmus was the first to get out of his car, followed by a mid-fifties white man with a long beard and a moustache and wearing a black overcoat. The man gestured to Dr Erasmus to follow him into the house, which Dr Erasmus obliged.

Seconds later, Dr Erasmus and his escort entered the large living room of the farmhouse, and they found two other people – middle-aged men of more or less the same age as them, both of them also wearing black overcoats. They were sitting around a wooden lodge table in the centre of the living room.

Both Dr Erasmus and his escort did not wait for an invitation to join the two sitting men, nor did they bother with greetings. They just quietly sat down. They knew one another, and their purpose for being here.

With everybody sitting comfortably in their seats, and ready for the meeting to start, one of the men who had already been seated when Dr Erasmus entered the room, cleared his throat and said, "Gentlemen, we are all here. Introductions are neither needed nor desirable. I, therefore, ask that we observe a strict protocol of not referring to each other by names, nicknames or anything that can identify us, in case anyone is listening. I have, of course, taken the necessary precautions about the latter point. But you never know. I suggest that we identify one another by numbers – kind of like how they do it when setting commission discussion groups. I am 'Number One'..."

Dr Erasmus volunteered to take Number Two, and the other men became Number Three and Number Four, respectively. When they were done selecting their identifying numbers,

Number One said, "Thank you, gentlemen, for your understanding. Number Two, I trust that your trip was incident free?"

"Indeed, it was Number One, thank you," Dr Erasmus said.

"Quite. Now to business. As you know the President has had another meeting with the jailed Nelson Mandela. It is looking quite likely that he will soon be released. The ANC is also making preparations for political negotiations. Their position is set out in the so-called Harare Declaration. Number Two, you have a better view of this situation. Fill us in please," Number One said.

"Your summation is correct Number One. I have just come from London, and I met with some of the key leaders of the ANC. They are preparing to come home. The President is making plans, which are quite advanced, for all this to happen. I suspect that he will use his annual address to Parliament to advance this," Dr Erasmus said.

"Very well. We must proceed with our plans. Number Three, give us your report," Number One said.

"We are ready, Number One. We have enough yield for three devices, construction is all but complete. The devices are ready for inspection downstairs," Number Three said.

"Anything to add, Number Four?" Number One asked.

"I concur with Number Three, Sir. We are good to go," Number Four said.

"Very well, then. Let me also indicate that the American CIA is snooping around. They don't trust the report of the IAA, which as you know has formally rendered the Pelindaba project moribund. I'm concerned about the fact that the Americans have superior detection equipment and will definitely find this material you have in your downstairs in no time. What do you think Number Two?" Number One asked.

"I agree, Number One, the stuff can't be kept here. Kimberley is a big city now and attracts all types. I suggest we move the stuff in phases. First, we move it to Farm Sixteen. Once there, customised encasings must be done for long-term haulage and storage," Dr Erasmus said.

"I agree," said Number Four, butting in, and continued, "there is a lot of trucking traffic in the area. We can get our own truck, customise and design it for the second phase of movement, without being detected."

"Indeed. Farm Sixteen is only temporary. It too will become a significant place of interest, especially to the ANC. We must take the stuff to the sea, where it's cooler. I have already made arrangements in this regard. Near the PE Harbour, there is a disused underwater bunker, in the Humewood area. I have already made adjustments to it such that it accommodates the devices. I suggest that we make the casings to be watertight," Number One said.

"But a harbour is a public place, with heavy traffic and witnesses. How has this been factored?" Dr Erasmus asked.

"Well, Number Two, all the witnesses have been taken care of, if you know what I mean. And the guards who will be on duty when the stuff arrives will too be taken care of," Number One said.

"I see, OK," Dr Erasmus said and continued, "and Tiaan and his men are ready to provide security."

"But we also need an on-ground tactical leader for this mission. Someone we can trust. Is there someone like that in your office, Number Two?" Number One asked.

"Yes, my head of Special Operations, Brigadier Elize Theron. She's a player," Dr Erasmus said.

"Very well. I agree. What is our sleeper time?" Number One asked.

"It's ten years," Dr Erasmus replied.

"Why ten years, if I may ask?" Number Four asked.

"Well, we figure the ANC must first be rendered normal. At the moment it is too saint-like. It can do no wrong and attacking it in the manner we're proposing would be counterproductive at best. We need a period of embedding failure. You will appreciate I can't say any more than that," Dr Erasmus said.

"Thank you for the explanation, Number Two," Number Four said.

"Number Three, can the devices stay underwater for ten years and remain functional?" Number One asked.

"Yes, but any longer than that, the material will start to deteriorate," Number Three replied.

"Triggering is done by remote as we agreed, right?" Number One asked.

"Yes, Number One," Number Four replied.

"We shall need two triggering devices; one must be kept by Number Two, and the other by me," Number One said.

"It shall be done, in the next seven days," said Number Three.

"Very well. Now let us go and inspect Three and Four's facility, shall we?" Number One said.

The four men around the table stood up almost in unison. With Number Three leading, they all went to an adjacent room, where Number Three opened a trapdoor on the floor, which led to a well-lit basement. Like everything else in this house, the basement was large. The walls were fitted with garage tool boards on which hung an impressive array of tools, some of which were rare and not available in the open market in South Africa. At the centre of the basement, there were three wooden tables, on top of which were three wire laden contraptions with a black oval-shaped metal rod at the centre.

"How long did you say it will you take a finish up here?" Number One asked.

"Give or take three days. The hard part is done. All that needs to happen now is encasing," Number Four said.

"What do you need?" Number One asked.

"We have most of what we need. But for transit purposes, I'd say we need coffin-sized metallic boxes," Number Three said.

"Alright. Is there anything else, Number Two?" Number One asked.

"Yes. There are two other contingencies that may need to hitch a ride on this plan. But rather let me call you about it later. The necessary preparations are being concluded," Dr Erasmus said.

"Alright, I'll await your call then. Coordinate with Number Three and Number Four on these other contingencies. We are done, for now, Gentlemen," Number One said.

And just like that, the four men left the basement and went to their cars and left the smallholding, without a single word to each other. Dr Erasmus did not bother going to a hotel. He just got into his car and drove straight back to Pretoria. But driving back provided him with an opportunity to think and evaluate the meeting he just came out of.

Besides being tired, Dr Erasmus was satisfied. Progress towards the goals of Project Echo was being attained systematically. The people he had just met were the central figures in this project. The two people who had tagged themselves as Number Three and Number Four were, in fact, nuclear physicists working on a dirty bomb to fight against the betrayal of the white folks, which the President's draft speech was portending. The other man who had tagged himself as Number One was, in fact, Colonel Hein Terblanche, working under an assumed name of 'Mr Peter Weir', a former soldier who spent years fighting against SWAPO at the South West Africa /Angola border. He was the designated leader of Project Echo, with Dr Erasmus providing tactical and strategic intelligence.

Dr Erasmus was also very aware that his dealings with the likes of General Kloppers were a bona fide act of disloyalty to the state and to the President. He knew that, were it to be found out that he had a secret rendezvous with people conspiring to resist the President's political program, he would be sent to jail for a long time, if lucky to escape an assassin's bullet.

But he despised the National Party and its leadership and regarded them as weak, so much so that he felt any fear he had of what they would do to him was far superseded by the need to act against their betrayal of the white folk. As far as he could see it, the ANC was mouthing nonracialism at the moment, making as if race doesn't matter where they're concerned. But Dr Erasmus was convinced that as soon as the ANC comes into power, it would be the turn of white people to be oppressed. Everything he learned about the ANC suggested to him that the ANC is as racist as in its propagation of black issues as the National Party was about white issues. The only difference was that the National Party knew it was racist, while the ANC was in denial, pending its ascent to power, and as far as he was concerned, this reality justified the treacherous behaviour he was embarking upon.

***

Dr Erasmus arrived back in Pretoria at about 11 o'clock in the morning. He was as tired as a dog. The only sleep he had in the last twenty-four hours was on the plane from London. Driving to and from Kimberley had been the craziest thing he had done in a long time, but he reckoned it could not be helped and was happy he had done it.

As soon as he arrived at his house at Waterkloof, he briefly greeted his wife, but refused to engage in any elongated conversations. All he did was to ask her to take out the children's presents which were still in the boot of the car and dish them out herself to the children as soon as they came back from an errand in the area. After that, he asked not to be disturbed, and went to their bedroom, looking forward to nothing but a good, long sleep.

***

Six hours later, at just after five o'clock in the afternoon, Dr Erasmus was woken up by the telephone ringing on his bedside stand. He cursed himself for not disconnecting the damn thing. He picked it up, quite like something he could throw away.

It was Marius Kleinfeldt, head of security at the Reserve Bank. The realisation made Dr Erasmus be fully awake at once. Marius was part of a team he had quietly been setting up for the last few years to manage certain aspects of the President's very near future intentions. In particular, Marius had been tasked with securing what he and fellow team members called 'folk assets', and as the head of security in the Reserve Bank, his task was to redirect on a gradual scale, gold stockpiles for safekeeping elsewhere.

With a degree of hesitation, he answered, "Yes, Mr Kleinfeldt, what can I do for you?"

"Doc, I saw the President's draft parliamentary speech. Don't ask me how, but we need to talk," Marius said.

"Right now?" Dr Erasmus asked.

"Yes, if you don't mind, Doc," Marius said.

"Alright, let's meet at your house in one hour. Is that OK?" Dr Erasmus asked.

"Yes, that's fine, Doc," Marius said.

"See you in an hour then," Dr Erasmus said, and the conversation ended.

An hour later, Dr Erasmus arrived at the Faerie Glen house of Mr Marius Kleinfeldt. Situated in a cul de sac and surrounded by tall Jacaranda trees, the house was a sprawling single-story

Balinese mansion, and as he drove up the driveway, Dr Erasmus marvelled at how secluded it was.

Not long after parking his car in the paved driveway, Marius emerged from inside the house and cheerfully said, "Ah, there you are Doc! Welcome. You can leave your car here."

Moments later, the two gentlemen were sitting in Marius's study. With prior knowledge of Dr Erasmus's drinking preferences, Marius had already poured two glasses of whiskey on the rocks for both of them.

"Well, Mr Kleinfeldt, what is going on?" Dr Erasmus asked as he grabbed his glass of whiskey, not wanting to waste any time with small talk.

"I should ask you that question, Doc. What is going on?" Marius asked, and gestured for Dr Erasmus not to answer, and continued, "What I see in the President's draft is disconcerting, to say the least. Our people went through periods of untold strife, and in what is being proposed, I see us returning to suffering. The concentration camps of the Anglo-Boer War and the problem of poor whites during the 1930s will be like a picnic. We can't do this!"

"Mr Kleinfeldt, we are past the stage of 'ifs'. We have discussed these matters before. Lamentations serve no purpose at this point. Only action is needed," Dr Erasmus said, unsympathetically.

"Alright Doc, I guess I'm panicking. Up to this point, the whole thing has been existing in the realm of theory," Marius said.

"But why did you ask me here?" Dr Erasmus pressed.

"There is an investigation coming up. I'm concerned I won't be able to escape it," Marius said quietly.

"What are they looking at?" Dr Erasmus asked.

"The stocks are not reconciling. What do you expect? So, they're looking at everything, and at everybody. I can't take a lie detector test Doc," Marius said.

"I see. Is there anything you're proposing should be done?" Dr Erasmus asked.

"Well, yes. They're going to search my house. I don't know when, but it will be soon. I want the stuff out of my house as soon as possible," Marius said, getting agitated.

"Alright, Mr Kleinfeldt, can I see the stuff?" Dr Erasmus said, continuing, "I've only heard about this from you, but I never actually confirmed anything."

"Well, today's your lucky day then, Doc. Come this way," Marius said and gestured for Dr Erasmus to follow him to an adjacent room, which looked like a children's computer room. Marius sat down behind one computer, typed a few keys on the keyboard, and then stood up, saying, "Watch and learn Doc."

To the amazement of Dr Erasmus, the lights in the computer room became dim, and then there was a whooshing sound as what had looked to Dr Erasmus like a normal room dividing wall, suddenly slid sideways, revealing a brightly lit room with what looked like a private bank box room, with rows of metallic drawers.

"It's all there, Doc. I never took even a single bar for myself," Marius said, pulling open one of the metal drawers. Inside there were neatly packed one-kilogram gold bars, which Dr Erasmus knew had been stolen from the Reserve Bank over a period of time.

Dr Erasmus, with his face deadpan, asked, "Roughly how much do you think this is worth?"

"I'd say about four billion rands," Marius said quietly.

"Alright, Mr Kleinfeldt, within the next 24 hours, the material will be removed from your house," Dr Erasmus said.

"Thank you, Doc," Marius said.

"Now, if there is nothing else ..." Dr Erasmus said.

"There is nothing else Doc, except to say that I fully understand the implications of what I'm saying," Marius said.

"Very well. I hope it will not get to that. I'll call you to arrange access to your house," Dr Erasmus said, as he stood up to leave.

As Marius was busy closing the drawer he had opened for Dr Erasmus, he suddenly felt a stinging sensation in his neck. Thinking that maybe he had been bitten by a mosquito, his hand reached instinctively to the itching part of his neck. It felt wet, and the horror of what happened dawned on him as he saw his hand dripping with his own blood. He looked accusingly at Dr Erasmus, as he saw him standing near the door, with a silenced gun in his hand. But before he could ask why, Marius fell to the floor and died.

A few seconds later, back in his car, Dr Erasmus made a call to a number he had on speed-dial, and said, "Mr Kleinfeldt is checked out. Send a team to his house to retrieve the material, and to clean up, tonight."

There was no response from the person on the other side of the line. But Dr Erasmus knew that the message had been received, and he sped off the property.

* * *

As Dr Erasmus was leaving Marius Kleinfeldt's house, he decided to make a call on his car phone to a long-time 'friend'.

"*Hola* Mnce!" he said as soon as his friend answered. Speaking *tsotsi taal*, or at least a poor version of it, was something he did only when speaking to Mncedisi Mmango, because Mncedisi always spoke in a colloquial way, and to get through to him, one had to do likewise. Dr Erasmus always found it strange a master's degree from Wits University had had no effect on Mncedisi's street lingo, and that instead, it was rubbing off on him.

"Hola Doc, *hoezit my broer?*" Mncedisi replied cheerfully.

"*Ke moja* my man!" Dr Erasmus replied, feeling silly.

"So, what's up, Doc?" Mncedisi asked, feeling keen to get to the reasons for this call.

"Man, let's hook up at Menlyn, now if you can. I'll be at the Wimpy," Dr Erasmus said.

"Sure thing Doc. *Ngiyazwakala,*" Mncedisi said, and the conversation ended.

About an hour later, Dr Erasmus was joined by Mncedisi Mmango at Wimpy, Menlyn Centre. True to form, Mncedisi came through the entrance with a well-defined swag. He was wearing tight-fitting jeans, a pair of black All-Star shoes, a red striped t-shirt and a navy blue London Fog jacket. He looked anything but the community leader he held himself to be.

"What will you have? I'm starving," Dr Erasmus said as soon as Mncedisi arrived at his table.

"Yes, Doc me too, *broer.* I'm so hungry I can eat a horse! I'll have six hundred grams of steak, medium to rare, with chips and a glass of wine," Mncedisi said.

"Good, I think I'll have the same. Now, about why I called you here," Dr Erasmus said, and paused, and looked at Mncedisi sternly, and continued, "Jokes aside. Project Echo is about to enter a new phase. Be ready," Dr Erasmus said, looking serious.

"*Eish* Doc, do you still need me for this?" Mncedisi said.

Much as Dr Erasmus had not expected the question, he was immediately ready to put the need of asking it ever again, down for good, by saying "Mr Mmango, this is a blood in, blood out arrangement. It's not a civil service job, where you get to retire into the sunset." He paused, and looked straight at Mncedisi's eyes, before continuing, "You know that I'm the keeper of your sins. Do what I ask of you, or I shall confess your sins on your behalf. Even if the ANC forgives you for betraying its cadres, I assure you, you will not recover from the publication of that information.

Furthermore, we know that you killed your girlfriend, and we know where you buried her. One tip to the police will send you to jail for over thirty years – that is if you escape the death penalty. So, let's not be asking academic questions here, Mr Mmango."

"So it's clear Doc, *ang'na* choice!" Mncedisi said.

"You don't. Now, here's what's going to happen. Everything is going to be done to guide your growth, such that when Echo reaches maturity, ten years from now, you will be ready to assume an important leadership role," Dr Erasmus said and paused, with his face unreadable. He opened the zip of his lumber jacket, revealing the butt of his gun, which was protruding menacingly under his arm, and before Mncedisi could say anything, he continued, "Let me be very frank, however. We will keep a close watch on you, and should you deviate to any extent from the path we have chosen for you, we will not hesitate to cancel your subscription to Project Echo. And so I ask you Mr Mmango, do you accept this mission?"

Mncedisi, now with all the jocularity in his demeanour gone, looked at Dr Erasmus contemplatively and then said, "I accept."

"Very well," Dr Erasmus said and zipped his lumbar jacked up again, and continued, "Now, tonight I shall open an offshore account for you, into which I shall deposit an amount of one million rand for you, and for the other guys. You agree with that?"

"Who are the other guys, Doc?" Mncedisi asked.

"You will know them when you need to know them. Right now, you don't need to know," Dr Erasmus said.

"Alright, I agree, Doc," Mncedisi said.

"Quite. Let's change the subject. I see our food has arrived. Let's eat," Dr Erasmus said, and continued, "Do you think Orlando Pirates will ever score a goal this season?"

In the coming days, Dr Erasmus repeated the same matters he addressed with Mncedisi Mmango in subsequent telephone calls and meetings over a period of three days with sixteen other similar types of people, after which he took their details in order to facilitate offshore deposits of R1 million per person.

The Bloody Speech

It is often said that not all days are alike, that sometimes what each day portends is reflected in how it makes us feel when we wake up. The 2nd of February 1990 was one such day. At just after midday, the day was hot, with the full glare of the sun sternly focused on Pretoria. In fact, the SA Weather Bureau had earlier reported that today's temperatures in Pretoria would reach a maximum of 43 degrees Celsius.

Every air conditioning system in the city was humming on overdrive, in a futile attempt to tame the scorching Pretoria sun. Most people, those not lucky enough to be inside air-conditioned buildings, were walking up and down the busy Strubens Street in downtown Pretoria, with most of them carrying umbrellas or wearing wet handkerchiefs on their heads to keep from dehydrating.

The sky was clear as far as the eye could see, with a hazy mirage hovering over the city's distant horizon, and not a single bird was venturing out from the shades of rooftops and the Jacaranda trees.

Yet the heat notwithstanding, there was no sense of anyone being subdued by the weather. If anything, there was a general air of excitement around, because the President was expected to make a big speech in Parliament that afternoon. The city streets, most of them one-ways, were a hive of activities. Newspaper vendors were making a bristling trade, often calling on passers-by, *'Mandela will be free today! The ANC is coming back! Read all about it in the papers. I have the Pretoria News, the Star, the Sowetan, zonke bonke!'*

Even though by far the majority of the city's residents regarded this particular President as not theirs, somehow everybody just had a sense of momentous change in prospect as a result of the speech he was due to make that afternoon. This expectation of good things from the speech seemed to propel the President into a realm of acceptance, even legitimacy of sorts, and because of that, people seemed to have put everything on hold in order to listen to him.

The United Democratic Front, the Congress of South African Trade Unions and a host of organisations aligned to the Mass Democratic Movement, had also earlier issued statements to the effect that people must listen to the speech of the illegitimate President, after which they must go to the street to either celebrate or protest. Analysts across a range of media platforms were appearing on TV and asking ad nauseam – was the speech going to live up to its billing, was it going to be another Rubicon fiasco? Was it going to be the damp squib some were predicting it would be? Would Mandela finally be released from prison? Would the ANC be unbanned? What reform prospects lay in store?

These and numerous other questions were also being asked, albeit with an entirely different kind of angle and anxiousness, in a rather nondescript building in downtown Pretoria. The decrepit and none too shabby eight-story building was snuggled among a cluster of buildings housing several *mashonisa* schemes as well as a number of charismatic churches which had a rather nasty habit of holding noisy mass every day of the week.

Perhaps because of the high number of civil servants working in buildings in the area, the place was also very popular with lower end prostitutes. In fact, if you listened closely, even in this heat, you could hear prostitutes briskly conducting negotiations with their clients in the street, even in front of this building's rather obscure entrance.

Looking at the façade of the building from a distance, you would never guess that anything of importance is taking place in it. But of course, to those in the know, who were preciously few, this was the headquarters of the Special Operations Division of the National Intelligence Service, known simply as 'the SOD', under the command of the 47-year-old Brigadier Elize Theron. A row of satellite dishes and antennas on the building's rooftop, as well as the unusually alert security guards at the gate and the reception area, gave the game away – that this was not a usual building, and the high perimeter fence, with mesh wiring at the edges completed its foreboding look.

Up on the eighth and final floor, Brigadier Elize Theron, whom we shall refer to from here on simply as Elize, was absent-mindedly chewing on her pen and aimlessly swivelling about in her office desk chair. The panoramic view of the city from her office, including the Union Buildings, the University of South Africa and the Voortrekker Monument in the distance, did not seem to have any effect on her brooding mood.

She was also not in the least concerned about Pretoria's heatwave. She looked grim and judging by her tightly furrowed brow, you could tell that she was deeply buried in thoughts that clearly didn't seem to be happy ones. This outlook was further complemented by the fact that today she was wearing clothes that made her look rather like a prison matron, with a longish brown skirt, dark pair of pantyhose, shiny semi high-heeled black shoes, and a white open-necked shirt.

Her desk was clean, with absolutely no piece of paper on it, perhaps betraying a neat freakish personality. In a corner adjacent to the desk, there was a portable flagpole on which hung South Africa's post union flag. On all the walls of the rather large office hung portraits of the white establishment leaders, from FW de Klerk, PW Botha right up to Verwoerd, JBM Hertzog, and Jan Smuts.

Elize's diminutive stature and unassuming appearance belied the fact that she was, in fact, a veteran of the SADF's numerous cross border raids and several skirmishes with the liberation forces of South Africa, who had also seen action against SWAPO at the then Caprivi Strip in Namibia, as well as in Angola against FAPLA, among other things.

Elize had been a soldier with the South African Defence Force since she was eighteen years. In the twenty-nine she spent with the army, almost fifteen years of those were spent in Military Intelligence.

In all that time, even at the height of their strength before the disastrous encounter with the Cubans at Cuito Cuanavale, she had always known that this day would come. All the data she and her team of spooks at MI looked at, sometimes complemented by personnel from the NIS, suggested that their struggle to maintain white supremacy in South Africa was a lost cause.

For a moment, with one television analyst giving a tiring assessment of the day's events, Elize pondered this issue of the white establishment trying to maintain whatever tenuous hold it had over the last three centuries in this part of the world. Nothing seemed to work, she thought ruefully. In about a week from today, South West Africa would gain its independence, bringing the South West Africa People's Organisation, Pretoria's arch-enemy, into power. All the sanctions-busting activities they had undertaken, had come to nought, with local businesses pleading with the state to reach an understanding with the banned

ANC, with some of them even treacherously going to Lusaka to meet with the ANC leadership.

There was nothing they had not tried to destroy the ANC itself, including cross border raids, mass detentions, torture, targeted assassinations, deep infiltration, etc. But as of this moment, the organisation seemed to have acquired more strength, especially in the hearts and minds of the majority black population.

Committed as she was to the fight against terrorism and to the cause of maintaining white supremacy, Elize understood the prevailing balance of forces very well, which was why she supported President FW de Klerk's attempts to reach out to the jailed Nelson Mandela, and to the steps he was about to announce in Parliament that afternoon. She also had sympathy with the white business establishment that was pleading for a break from the effects of sanctions.

One of her colleagues, a Colonel Brian van der Berg, whose office was two stories down, walked into the office and in the process disturbed Elize's train of thought. Wearing a brown suit with faint black stripes, Brian looked nonchalant if not with a bit of airs in his demeanour. Clearly, he was very familiar with Elize. He too had a long service with the SADF, he too had served much of his time in the SADF with Military Intelligence, and they both transferred at the same time to civilian intelligence under the auspices of the National Intelligence Service.

Brian did not greet or do any other pleasantries. He just came in and lunged for the television remote control that was on Elize's desk, and increased the volume just as President FW de Klerk was saying:

"The steps that have been decided are the following:

The prohibition of the African National Congress, the Pan Africanist Congress, the South African Communist Party and a number of subsidiary organisations is being rescinded ..."

"What the fuck!" Brian exclaimed, looking at the TV as if he could just punch it. "Tell me this is not happening!" Brian continued as he pulled a chair to make himself comfortable.

"Well, it is," said Elize, rather coolly.

"*Magtig man! Ek kan hierdie ding regtig nie glo nie*! How can FW just hand over the country to terrorists just like that!" Brian thundered with his rough baritone voice.

"Well, as they say, there's no point in crying over spilt milk. It is what it is," Elize said, with a heavy sigh of resignation.

"But how are we supposed to play this from now on? Do you even support this?" Brian asked, still confused.

"The way I see it, every situation, no matter how bleak it may seem at first, ultimately has its benefits, at least that's my attitude at the moment," said Elize matter of factly.

"But Elize, what benefits could there be in this situation? FW is unleashing the ANC and its communist *broers* on us! How can any good come of that? I mean, unless I'm mistaken, this unbanning of the ANC means there is going to be one man one vote. It's a matter of time. It means there will never be a whites-only government again. It means there may never even be a white person in any leadership position in this country, ever again. And more ominously, it means white suburbs are going to be swamped by *kaffirs*! It means white folk will die through inbreeding induced attrition. It means the Afrikaans language, which the ANC already regards as the language of the oppressor, will die, with our folk being force-fed a diet of kaffir languages. It means our universities, our schools and our churches will be taken over by bands of marauding *impis*! Imagine our people being attended to in hospitals by angry kaffir doctors! So please Brigadier Theron, with the greatest of respect, please enlighten me about how any of this may be of benefit to us!" Brian asked, with a seething and preachy tone of voice.

"Your problem, Brian, is that your thinking is crude. It always has been. You think every problem will be solved by *skiet* and *donner*. We have tried all that as you very well know," Elize said, with a stern but patient tone of voice.

"But still ..." Brian mumbled

"But nothing," Elize said, cutting him off, and continued, "as I see it, this problem requires the laying of long-term plans, not the brash reiteration of tired racist ideologies. This is a whole new ball game. Anyway, we have to cut this chit chat. In the next five hours, I'm attending a special meeting of the State Security Council. Some of this planning I'm talking about maybe ventilated there. I have to prepare for a possible presentation."

"Sure thing, ma'am. Anything you want me to do in the meantime?" Brian asked.

"Well, this is going to be a long day. I don't know how long the SSC is going to be. I'll call you if there's a need to meet afterwards," Elize said, once again returning to her reflective pose, and effectively dismissing Brian from her office.

"Yes, ma'am," Brian said, with a faint salute as he left the room.

Seeking Assurance

At about quarter to six that afternoon, more or less two hours after the President had tabled his speech in Parliament, Elize arrived at the Union Buildings for a meeting that was scheduled to start at six o'clock. Even though she arrived fifteen minutes before time, it had been a struggle. Almost all the roads in the city centre were heavily congested, not with traffic, but with throngs of people that had come out to celebrate the unbanning of political organisations, which had earlier been announced in Parliament by President FW de Klerk.

Under normal circumstances, the Pretoria traffic is easier to navigate than most other cities in South Africa, even on a Friday when everybody is rushing out to faraway destinations. Part of the reason for this is the number of large one-way streets, which make it easier to connect from one street to the next, even in instances of a power failure induced traffic jam.

But today it was gridlock from every direction, caused by the numbers of people in the street. In every street, and all along the main Church Street, the excitement was palpable. The police, instinctively knowing that their usual heavy-handedness in suppressing gatherings would not work today, were standing by, seemingly content to watch even as some of the activists started to drape the statue of Paul Kruger in ANC colours.

People were excitedly waving the previously banned flags of the ANC and the SACP, punctuated with fervent shouts of "*amandla!*" Everywhere there were banners, some hanging on the balconies of nearby buildings, carrying messages such as Viva ANC! Viva ANCYL! Viva ANCWL! *Mayibuye iAfrika!* Freedom or Death, Victory is Certain! UDF Unites, Apartheid Divides!

The air was made even more electric by the powerfully rendered freedom songs, with "*siyaya ePitoli*" and "*Nelson Mandela sabela uyabizwa*" the dominant ditties. At times they would stop singing altogether and listen to impromptu speeches from the leadership of the UDF and COSATU, which they would follow with powerful stomping of the ground, doing the "toyi-toyi" –a physically exerting guttural cry-and-response rhythm, mimicking the military training of MK and ZIPRA guerrillas.

Alone in a nondescript Toyota Corolla, Elize was listening to reports of similar scenes across the country. As she was patiently trying to navigate through this mound of humanity, her mind was wondering what lay ahead for the country. Many a time they, in the security establishment, had talked about "Day X" – the day when the ANC army, uMkhonto we Sizwe, accompanied by its communist allies would break through all their defences and march victoriously on Pretoria. The scenes she was witnessing seemed to be fast approaching this scenario, although not quite there yet.

***

Looking decidedly flustered and clearly bothered, when Elize finally arrived at the Union Buildings she took a deep sigh of relief as she parked her car along Fairview Avenue. With a brisk sense of purpose in her step, she walked into the street level reception area of the Union Buildings, where she was immediately processed and directed to where the meeting of the State Security Council was set to take place.

She had been through this process on numerous occasions in the past and was quite familiar with the reception personnel, but for the first time in as long as she could remember, Elize took a brief moment to actually look at this place – the all-white security personnel at the entrance, the long stone steps, the stone-paved driveway on which a string of luxury sedans were parked, and another set of steps leading to the west wing entrance, where another security station was located.

From there, the security took her to Cabinet boardroom 159. As she arrived at the boardroom, she found that other people were already there, waiting for the meeting to start. With about five minutes left before the meeting would start, she had just about enough time to help herself to coffee that was on offer near the entrance of the boardroom.

With her cup of coffee and pastries in hand, Elize took her seat, about eight seats away from the Chairperson's seat. Quickly panning around the room, she could recognise all the faces in the room, including those whose faces were never seen in public.

Seated at the top of the table as Chair of the meeting was the Minister of Justice. Next to him was the Minister of Law & Order, followed by the Minister of Defence, and the Minister of Prisons. The rest of the seats were taken by the top brasses of both the military and the police, including the Chief of the Defence Force, the Chief of the Army, the Chief of the Navy, the Chief of the Air Force and the Chief of Military Intelligence. The Commissioner of the SA Police and police divisional heads took up the rest of the seating space. Elize and the Director-General of the NIS, Dr Hans Erasmus were the only ones from civilian intelligence.

The mood in the room was sombre, Elize quickly noticed. Ordinarily, these were people who were trained never to display any emotion in public. But today they were barely holding their tears. Whereas they would normally be sharing jokes, mostly at their own expense, and laughing at all sorts of things, today everyone was looking down and doing their best to hide their faces.

From the chair, the Minister of Justice broke this morose air in the room, thundering gruffly, *"Dames en here, hierdie vergadering sal tot orde kom*! As you can see, the President is not here. He is engaged in urgent consultations with many leaders in Europe and America, and he has asked me to chair this meeting on his behalf. We have one item on the agenda: 'The Security Implications of The President's speech'. I know that all of you here were consulted in advance of the President's speech. So, let none of us pretend that we did not know. Of course, now that the speech has been delivered, we may be seeing aspects of its implications we did not anticipate. We must not beat ourselves up about this. We must think and offer practical solutions. It's clear that the game has changed, and the question is how we must play it going forward. I don't want us to be here longer than is necessary. We have a lot of work to do. The developments announced today by the President have a built-in self-propelling momentum, against which we must seek to have insurance. Therefore, on behalf of the rest of government, I'm here to ask you, in your sections, to design plans that accommodate and respond to the reality that white people are now more than likely to live under a black majority government. There are no specific terms of reference other than the emphasis that what the President announced has our support, but in being prudent with the future of the white folks, I am asking all of you to present to me in the next 48 hours, plans that reflect assurances. So, in this meeting, I want to hear what you understand the situation to be, and what your plans are about it."

After the opening by the Chairperson, everybody around the room started to give their views of what was happening in the country from their various perspectives. The Minister of Defence started by saying, "Well Chairperson, the situation with the homelands is hard to read at the moment. The Transkei has definitely gone rogue. It has MK and APLA training camps. At the moment we are just watching the situation. We don't know how many soldiers the ANC has, but we estimate that not to be more than fifteen thousand. We are also keeping watch on weapons movement into the country. The unbanning is likely to be used as an opportunity to increase forward deployments, especially by MK and APLA, until a formal integration method is adopted. Already they are saying whatever negotiations may take place they must be accompanied by sustained mass action – what they call 'the Leipzig option'. We also have another problem. The CIA is putting pressure on us to dismantle the Pelindaba program. They don't want these weapons to fall into the hands of people such as Gaddafi and Fidel Castro. The International Atomic Agency is in the country already, to start their inspection of our facilities. The KwaZulu homeland is also very tricky. We think they will push very hard for the recognition of the chiefs and will do anything in this regard. Another area of great concern at the moment is the mobilisation of far-right organisations led by the AWB."

When everybody was done talking, about an hour later, the Chairperson then said, "Well ladies and gentlemen, I have heard you. I will report your views to the President. In the meantime, as we adjourn, I want all of you to go and develop proper plans taking into account everything you have just said. I don't know when the next meeting of the SSC will be, but I suspect we might need to call a special one within a week. We are adjourned."

***

As she drove back from the Union Buildings, Elize was not sure what to make of the SSC meeting, or for that matter, whether it should have been called at all. The meeting had not lasted more than an hour. By seven o'clock, it was over. As she left the Union Buildings, it was dark, and the scorching sun had been replaced by an evening humidity. But Elize was thankful that at least the streets were now free from the earlier celebratory congestion.

She could now think, which was something she liked doing while driving. Certainly, there was a lot to think about concerning the SSC meeting. There were too many unspoken things, with too much being said only subliminally. There was an order to act, with no clear direction as to what that action must be specifically. Perhaps the SSC did not want to commit to acts that would be seen as undermining the President, by adopting a method of decision-making that allows for plausible deniability further down the line, she thought. What was clear, though, was that there was panic.

Since the "winds of change" speech delivered twenty-six years ago in 1960 by British Prime Minister Harold Macmillan, Afrikaners had always lived with the spectre of their proverbial Bastille being stormed. But today's speech by President FW de Klerk, spookily delivered on the 2nd of February, almost exactly as Macmillan's, which was delivered on 3 February 1960, sharply brought forward realities which had hitherto only been imagined.

Elize's train of thought was disrupted by a call she received from her boss, the 61-year-old Dr Hans Erasmus, the Director-General of the NIS.

"Elize, hi, do you have a moment?" Dr Erasmus asked.

"Sure thing, Doc, what's up?" Elize replied, assuming the same casual tone. Even though she and Dr Erasmus were not particularly close friends, they had long discarded official titles in their communication.

"Good, please swing by my place if you can, will you, now if you can. I know it's late, I apologise," Dr Erasmus said, and cut the line.

Without much thought, soon after this call, Elize immediately turned the car around and headed towards the direction of Pretoria East, where Dr Erasmus's house was located. Moments later, she arrived at Dr Erasmus's house, which was situated at Pretoria's Waterkloof suburb. Elize had been to this house before on consultation meetings with Dr Erasmus, but she could still not get over how beautiful and imposing it was. Built on a hilltop at Edward Street, the house was a vast property with sweeping views of Pretoria East.

As she slowly drove along the long, winding and floodlit cobblestone driveway, Elize briefly wondered about what Dr Erasmus had in mind. Calling on her to come over to his house would suggest that he had a specific operation in mind, at least if previous experience was anything to go by, she thought. Of course, she was alive to the very real possibility that if the speech of the President was the harbinger of change she thought it would be, Dr Erasmus would be among the first people to be directly affected. Was this a pressing of panic buttons? She wondered.

Again, her thoughts were interrupted by rather sharp, young and fit looking security personnel who suddenly appeared from the dark areas of the house and started to direct her to Dr Erasmus's basement study.

"Hi Doc, I must say your house looks splendid at night!" Elize said cheerfully as soon as she saw Dr Erasmus.

He was still wearing his work clothes, and with the tie still firmly tied on his neck, he did not look like he was home at all. His bearded face lit up at the sight of Elize standing at the doorway, and he said, "*Ag baie dankie,* Elize. It's the only place that centres my spirits at the moment, although I'm not sure if it is succeeding in doing that today. Come in, come in. Take a seat."

"Thank you, Doc," Elize said.

"I'm sure you are wondering why I called you here," Dr Erasmus said.

"The thought did cross my mind Doc, although I guess in the light of the day's events, I'm not really surprised," Elize replied.

"Well, we're in unknown territory now," Dr Erasmus said rather gloomily.

"Question is, what are we going to do about it?" Elize said, egging the Director-General on.

"You mean, what am I going to do? Well, I guess that's why I called you here. What will you have? I have beer, whiskey, orange juice, fizzy drinks, or I can get someone to bring us coffee?" Dr Erasmus said.

"Coffee will be fine, thanks. Black, with one teaspoon of sugar," Elize said.

"Very well then," Dr Erasmus said as he stepped outside to call on his helper for coffee, leaving Elize to look around the study, which had a large antique mahogany table at the centre, with seating for eight people. Half of the study's wall was fitted with wooden bookshelves, and directly behind Dr Erasmus's large swivelling chair was a giant South African flag. The rest of the wall was taken up by several framed academic certificates, including a BA Honours degree from the University of Stellenbosch, an MA from the University of Pretoria, a PhD from Oxford University, and a string of diploma certificates from a variety of institutions, both local and international.

About two minutes later, Dr Erasmus returned, and took up a seat directly opposite Elize, and said, "You were asking what we're going to do."

"Indeed, Doc. What are your thoughts on the President's speech?" asked Elize, keen to know why her boss had asked her here.

"Well, I think it's a decade too late! We wasted a lot of energy and resources fighting to preserve apartheid. But hey, we're here now. It had to be done, I guess," said Dr Erasmus, rather indignantly.

"What is the end game though?" Elize asked.

"Well, before we go any further with this, I want to make one point very clear – this discussion never took place, right?" Dr Erasmus said.

"What discussion?" Elize asked, suppressing a chuckle.

Dr Erasmus did not reply immediately. He looked at Elize with a lingering stare and then said, "Good. As you know, the SSC requires me, and others of course, to come up with a plan that will serve as insurance against the likely negative effects of what the President announced today. You were there, you heard them. You see, I support what the President has said, although as I say, I think it is ten years too late. Some of us in the security establishment have been arguing for quite some time that the ANC is not the kind of enemy you defeat in a shooting battle. The strength of the ANC is its popularity, not its military capability. Nothing else. And the basis of that popularity is the justness of its cause, at least in the eyes of the black majority. It's a more portent kind of strength, which has been helped immeasurably by our own repressive methods. The power of the liberation movement at this point in time is the glitter ordinary people see in its face. People love heroes and continuing with oppression strengthens that love. But ask yourself this – how does a hero sustain being a hero past victory? That is the strategic question motivating the President's speech."

"By dying?" Elize interjected, with incredulity.

"Yep. By dying. The hero must die after achieving a great victory, for the longer he lingers in life, the more his or her infallibility erodes. You see, in my view, the best way of fighting against a hero is to let the hero be in charge. That way you bring into reality the dynamic noted by Shakespeare's Henry IV when he says, 'Uneasy lies the head that wears the crown.'"

"Doc, I don't follow you. I never did like Shakespeare much. Those 'thous' and the 'shalts' just put me off," Elize said, laughing.

But before Dr Erasmus could reply, the helper, a middle-aged lady by the name of Gladys, walked in with a tray of coffee for both Dr Erasmus and Elize.

"Well, think about it. Between an Afrikaner who's handed over the responsibility of governing, and an ANC that assumes that responsibility, who is freer?" Dr Erasmus asked, caressing his cup of coffee.

"You're still not making any sense Doc!" Elize exclaimed.

Dr Erasmus sighed, and then said, "Well you asked earlier what the end game is. Let me put it this way, for the ANC, the end game is freedom day of course. To use their parlance, it's the beginning of the first phase of the National Democratic Revolution, with all the crap that goes with it! For the National Party, well so far as I can see, the National Party is likely to negotiate for group rights, minority rights, federalism, and anything that insulates much of the status quo. I don't see it working, and I don't think the government thinks it's gonna work either, which is why the Security Council is asking for assurance plans."

"Doc let me see if I get this. The National Party will hand over power to the ANC in the hope that the ANC will fail as a governing party, as a result of which it will lose its popularity? What guarantee does the National Party have of surviving post-ANC failures?" Elize asked.

Dr Erasmus replied with some alacrity, "None! In fact, it's a suicide mission for the National Party in its current form, although I will not tell them that, which is one of the reasons this discussion never took place! You see, this is the scenario – it's ten years after liberation. None of the promises has been met. There is restlessness abound in the country. The ANC begins to splinter. Its electoral fortunes begin to dwindle, and there is a desperate scramble to claw back lost support. Such a clawback will be premised largely on throwing money at the problem, until the money runs out."

"But what do you mean Doc?" Elize asked, puzzled.

Dr Erasmus replied, seemingly getting worked up, "I mean Elize, loss of political support for the National Party is not only inevitable but actually desirable. Think about it. Even though the ANC is in an alliance with communists, it is a nationalist organisation, in much the same way the National Party is. The only difference is that it hates racism. But it is as liberal and capitalistic as all the white parties."

"Pardon me Doc, but you're not making any sense! You may have missed it, but the ANC is not only demanding the end of racism. It is also talking about redistribution of the land and the nationalisation of what it calls the commanding heights of the economy. Surely that's not acceptable, no?" Eliza asked.

Dr Erasmus replied, "Maybe. But with Britain, Germany and the United States being the dominant players in the South African economy, how long do you think such rhetoric will last? The ANC knows this, or will soon know this, that to agitate these countries is a sure way of inviting early regime change, and the permanent disruption of their so-called 'stages of the National Democratic Revolution'. And so, all I'm saying is that the balance of forces has shifted such that the era of depending on the military to prop up a white government in Africa has ended. We can, of course, slog it out. But the outcome is a scorched earth, which would only introduce white folks to scales of strife and poverty they have never seen before, which can easily be avoided by foregoing racism ..."

"Unlike the black folks who are thoroughly experienced with living with strife and poverty! I see your point," Elize said, completing Dr Erasmus's sentence.

"Good. The sooner all of us in the security sector accept that, the sooner we will be able to think about alternatives," Dr Erasmus said.

"What alternatives can there be, though?" Elize asked.

Dr Erasmus replied rather emphatically, "My dear, this is the age of information, and the defeat of Russian communism means that this now is a unipolar world, dominated by the United States and its allies in Western Europe, all of whom have big long-term interests in South Africa. As such none of them will allow neither the establishment of communism nor the oppression of whites in South Africa. Besides, already the Americans are saying if we dismantle the Pelindaba project now, they will guarantee our people's interests long into the future. In other words, much as the ANC will run the government, it will not alter to any significant extent the basic structure of our society. The ANC will only broaden the existing template of governance. They will not alter it."

"So, allowing the ANC back into the country is an act of faith?" Elize asked, with a mischievous chuckle.

Dr Erasmus replied, "Yes. But we also have to take steps of our own to guarantee this. We must allow the enemy access into our lounge. Let him drink our fine scotch and eat our caviar. He'll grow fat and lazy and will develop a debilitating addiction. More importantly, the potency of his revolutionary ideas will be diluted by the comfort we will expose him to, and will ultimately be beholden to our interests, thus making it totally unnecessary for us to be actually in power. That's the idea."

"So, it's a battle of ideas?" Elize asked.

"You're not listening! In its Freedom Charter, the ANC already agrees with the notion of 'comfort'. It's the 'for all' part they need to lose. That's no battle!" Dr Erasmus said, with some enthusiasm.

"Ok, ok, back up a bit. I'm hearing you to be saying the South African Communist Party is not a threat, even though the ANC is aligned with it?" Elize asked.

Dr Erasmus replied, "Well, you know better than most that we spent years and inordinate amount of resources studying the ANC and the entire so-called liberation movement. Besides the end of the Cold War, another simple truth is that black people are not all that averse to capitalism. I seriously doubt that they would allow anyone to force them to queue for bread! The simple truth is that our anti-communist propaganda exaggerated the threat of communism."

"Doc, I'm in operations. I solve specific problems as and when they arise. Theory is really not my forte. But can I ask you though, is the President acting on your advice on these matters?" Elize asked.

"Pretty much yes," Dr Erasmus replied, coolly, and continued, "I have impressed on him that a retreating army is not a defeated army, that as a matter of fact, we are retreating in order to allow for the change we want to occur, and to be liberated from the burden of apartheid. The President certainly knows that allowing the ANC back into the country means loss of power by the National Party and loss of white privilege as we know it."

"And the emphasis is on 'as we know it', right?" Elize asked.

"Right," replied Dr Erasmus.

"Now what?" Elize asked.

"Tell me first, what is your operational assessment of the situation at the moment? You have better eyes than most of us," Dr Erasmus asked.

Elize replied, "Well Doc, there are a number of tasks that must be undertaken in the immediate future. These include opening the SADF bases to contain members of uMkhonto we Sizwe and APLA in anticipation of an integration process. We have to manage the re-entry of the ANC into the country, with a specific focus on the movement of their weapons. We also have to get the ANC to give us a list of all their security personnel. We must immediately start a process of managing all security information. Our shredders are ready. Overall, my prognosis is that the situation is flux and confused but manageable."

"I see, and I think you're correct. Now, enough about politics! Let me come to the reason why I called you here, and I'll go straight to it. You, and a few others, will not integrate into the new security establishment that is likely to come. I want you to retire formally, and I want your letter to this effect by end of business tomorrow. You do not need to know the reasons for this," Dr Erasmus said.

"OK, but what exactly do you want me to do?" Eliza asked.

Dr Erasmus stared at Elize for a while, as if trying to figure her out, and then said, "As you know, we have assets in the ANC. We must reveal something of them, on condition that nothing happens to them. But there are assets whose names are listed in an ultra-secret list – what we call the 'Master List'. Their names must never be revealed. There is an operation I want you to lead. It's called Project Echo, and its central objective is to permanently safeguard this list, together with a few other contingencies."

"Other contingencies Doc?" Elize asked.

"A lot of this is classified beyond your pay grade Elize. For now, you don't need to know," Dr Erasmus said.

"Ok but this list I'm supposed to safeguard, where is it?" Elize asked.

"First agree to my terms, then I'll tell what comes next," Dr Erasmus said, his face deadpan.

"Ok, so I resign tonight, and then do what?" Elize asked, prodding.

Dr Erasmus did not reply immediately. He stood up, went to a nearby filing cabinet and pulled a brown sealed envelope, and then said, "Go to Upington, first thing tomorrow morning. I suggest you drive. About forty kilometres outside Upington there is a small town called Klawer. Go there a day after arriving in Upington. There is a farm just about ten kilometres on the other side of Klawer, towards the Namibian border. It's a front for off radar NIS activities. It's called 'Farm Sixteen'. There you will be met by Captain Tiaan van Schalkwyk. He is commanding a special ops unit of a few men. Thread carefully. They will be suspicious of you. Once I have confirmed that you have made contact with him, I will send you further instructions. In fact, as you check-in at River City Hotel, the hotel concierge will hand you further instructions."

Elize sighed heavily and then said, "So that's it?"

Dr Erasmus again looked at Elize searchingly. He grabbed a black briefcase which had been by his side the entire time they'd been talking, and handed it to Elize, saying, "Yep, pretty much. I'm gonna give you cash so that you can manage your own logistics. I'll take your word for everything. No receipts and no paper of any kind must be generated from this op. There's two million rand in there in used two hundred-rand bills. There's going to be more as we go. We are done for now. Please leave all the agency's equipment issued to you at your house. Someone will go there to get it, together with your resignation letter. I'll call you if anything changes. You accept this mission?"

"How are you going to get the keys to my house?" Elize asked, not answering Dr Erasmus' question.

"You have a normal suburban house Elize. We do not need keys to enter a normal suburban house. Just leave the stuff in a place that's easy to find," Dr Erasmus said.

"Alright, one question though Doc. Why me? What makes you think I'll do this and never open my mouth about it?" Elize asked.

Dr Erasmus chuckled, not so much at what Elize was asking, but more at something he was thinking about. He stood up and reached behind his desk. From the top drawer of the desk he pulled out a black leather file, and then came back to sit next to Elize, and said, "This a dossier on all people whose disappearances we engineered over the years, you know, heroes of the revolution. This is evidence of who they were, coordinates of their unmarked graves, and more importantly, information on who put them there. When the ANC comes into power, they are going to want to know what we did with their people. This, therefore, my dear is some of the stuff a decision will have to be made on whether it should be handed over to the new ANC government, or not. *Moenie vir my toets nie,* Elize."

With her lips pouted as if she wanted to whistle, Elize let out a slow, "Yes, Doc, I accept, and even though I don't know how you propose to break into my house, I'll leave all the agency equipment on my dining room table."

"Very well. Let's end it here," Dr Erasmus said, and stood up to escort Elize to the door.

***

About an hour later, back in the comfort of her lounge at her Wonderboom house north of Pretoria, at about 10 o'clock in the evening, Elize poured herself a glass of scotch on the rocks, and as she threw herself on her leather couch, she let out a long sigh, punctuated by a hissing expletive. What the fuck did I just get myself into? she asked herself, with palpable futility. To her, right at that moment, it looked as if the world seemed to be conspiring to do her in, and there was nothing she could do about it.

With the Scotch swirling in her glass, she went over her conversation with Dr Erasmus again in her head. It was the strangest thing. She had known Dr Erasmus for quite some time, and all her interactions with him had been limited to cryptic instructions about this or that covert operation but had never been as substantive as this last interaction.

She had accepted Dr Erasmus's suggestion, (or was it an ultimatum?) to resign from her job with immediate effect, to go and do something that was decidedly not legal, partly because Dr Erasmus was correct in surmising her own operations background as something the coming ANC regime would be exceedingly unhappy with. She was aware of the nascent talk of a truth and reconciliation commission which would absolve sinners if they confessed. But she was loathed to subject herself to such kind of unburdening. There was just something wrong and shameful for a soldier to go down on all fours and beg for forgiveness, she thought bitterly. The people she'd killed, with whose exposure Dr Erasmus was now blackmailing her, had been declared enemies of the state, and it had been her duty to eliminate them. But explaining this to any future tribunal convened by the victorious enemy would not absolve her of culpability, and therefore existing on the sidelines and on the dark edges of the new society was a far better option than the shame of being spread-eagled on national television as the epitome of evil, she reckoned.

Another reason was simply that she was curious to know what Dr Erasmus was actually up to. But the fact that he was actually blackmailing her was exceedingly concerning. As far as she knew, intelligence officials at the level of Dr Erasmus tended to be concerned more with the outcomes of intelligence-gathering rather than the dirty craftsmanship of it. Why was Dr Erasmus risking his reputation by doing something so patently illegal? The thought made her grimace, and she closed her eyes, trying to shake off an uneasy feeling – that she might yet live to see this famous curiosity which is said to have taken the ninth life of the cat.

The Unknown Cargo

The following day, Elize left her house for what she prayed would not be the last time. Her letter of resignation, together with the NIS issued laptop, her state issue 9 mm-pistol, a box full of agency miscellaneous files, and keys to a BMW series 5 sedan. Again, she chuckled at the thought that someone was going to break in and get this, and mischievously shrugged the possibility that the stuff might actually be stolen by a genuine housebreaker!

She would not go to her office to say goodbye or collect her things; otherwise, this would defeat the purpose of the type of disengagement suggested by Dr Erasmus's plan. She accepted that all the management of her departure would be done by Dr Erasmus on her behalf.

At 3 am she was up, and cursing Dr Erasmus for suggesting that she must drive from Pretoria to Upington! After a quick shower, she put on her black and white Nike tracksuit, her flat-heeled and comfortable shoes suitable for long-distance driving, and a dark pair of glasses. After checking herself over in her bedroom mirror, she felt free and ready for the road.

At 4 am, driving her favourite Mercedes-Benz SLK 200, with its top down , Elize got onto the N1 highway and headed towards Bloemfontein. The morning breeze was refreshing, eliminating any lingering sleep she still had in her system.

Whatever confusion and fears she went to bed with last night, all had somewhat dissipated. Perhaps it was the sudden and unusual resignation from a job she had been doing for a number of years, or her eagerness to find out what the ultimate game of this trip was, but she felt at ease. Thinking about how long the trip to Upington was going to be, as she entered the N1 highway to Johannesburg, from where she would take the N8 towards the town of Upington, about 900 kilometres away, she pressed the accelerator.

***

That same day, at about one o'clock in the afternoon, after eight straight hours of driving, Elize arrived at the Northern Cape capital town of Upington. Tired and desperately needing to sleep off the effects of the long journey, she arrived at River City Inn at number 6 Park Street.

True to its reputation as the hottest place in South Africa, temperatures in Upington were hovering close to 46 degrees Celsius. The cool air in the hotel's reception was such a welcome relief, and before proceeding to the check-in counter, Elize poured herself a glass of ice-cold complimentary orange juice on a wooden stand near the counter.

With her thirst quenched, for now, Elize approached the check-in counter with her luggage in tow. As she was busy checking in, Monica, the lady receptionist said, "Oh, is your name Ms Elize Theron? I have a note here for you."

"For me?" Elize asked, remembering what Dr Erasmus had earlier said.

"Yep, here it is," Monica said cheerfully.

It was more than a note, Elize noted wryly, marvelling at Monica's sense of irony. This was, in fact, a large envelope, attached to a card box, which whatever it contained was more than a note! As soon as she got into her room on the third floor of the hotel, Elize opened the card box and found that there were a number of two-way radio "walkie talkies" as well as a handheld navigator.

Putting this box aside, Elize opened the envelope. There was a typed and unsigned letter, as well as an identity document. Curious, she read the letter, which did not have any greetings:

> "As you can see, there is an ID document that goes with this. This is now your new identity. As I said earlier, within the next twelve hours you must go to 'Farm 16', just outside the town of Klawer, in the north of the Cape Province, about 40 kilometres from here. Here are the coordinates: 38.9877N, 78.0360S. There you will meet with Tiaan van Schalkwyk and his team. There is a cargo of ten boxes. Their contents are not part of your mission, suffice to say, this is precious cargo, which includes matters pertaining to Project Echo, which we spoke about, and must be handled with care. When you arrive at Klawer, you will see that a special purpose truck has been procured in which the cargo must be loaded. Tiaan and his team, with you directing things, will drive the truck to the port of Port Elizabeth immediately after it has been loaded. On arrival at the PE Port, you will be met by a contact, under an assumed name of Peter Weir. The cargo will be loaded onto a fishing trawler named 'Good Mary', after which there will be further instructions. PS: This letter is written on self-burning paper and will automatically catch fire after ten minutes of exposure to light. Good luck."

Noting the latter point in the letter, Elize quickly looked at her watch and realised that she had less than a minute before the paper would burn in her hands. She grabbed the hotel's metal wastebasket and put the letter inside, taking care to move the wastebasket away from any incendiary material in the room. Sure enough, about thirty seconds later, there was a poof sound and then smoke, and the letter was done for.

With this drama out of the way, Elize looked at the ID document supplied with the letter. It had her picture, seemingly recently taken, and it said her new name is Martie Odendaal. She sighed, and decided to take a shower, after which she would call Captain Tiaan van Schalkwyk.

"Hi, Tiaan, its Martie Odendaal here. We have a mutual friend. I'm on my way. Get the stuff ready," Elize said as soon as Tiaan answered.

"It is ready," Tiaan replied with a soft voice that seemed rather nasal.

"Good. The time now is 15:05. I should be there within an hour, or less," Elize said.

"No, ma'am, I suggest you come after dark, say at eight," Tiaan replied, and Elize could sense his stern tone. It made her recall what Dr Erasmus had said about being careful with Tiaan and his team.

"Alright then, as you wish. See you at eight tonight," Elize said, relenting, and the line went dead.

Now she had time on her hands. Part of her had wanted to drive around the town and do some recceing of the place. But she didn't have the energy. Besides, the letter had given her a much clearer objective. She decided there was one thing she would do, and that was to visit some of the wine estates along the Orange River to buy wine.

***

As arranged with Tiaan, Elize arrived at 'Farm 16' at about eight o'clock in the evening. Driving slowly and cautiously, she arrived at the rusty farm gate that had a dry wooden board marked 'Mooi Plek'. The gate was closed although not locked. With a sigh of resignation, Elize got out of the car and pushed the gate wide open.

Even though it was dark, she could make out the light silhouette of the farmhouse. Further down the narrow gravel road from the gate, there were lights, which she slowly followed. About two hundred metres from the gate, the gravel road yielded to a parking lot made of concrete stones. Directly in front of the parking lot was the Dutch gabled main house of the farm.

Approaching slowly, Elize parked her car in the large concrete parkway just in front of the house and paused before getting out. And then she froze behind the car's steering wheel. A number of young men were filing out one by one from the shadows. They were armed. Even though they didn't have any guns out at the ready, Elize could see their underarm bulges.

They were young, not more than 19 years old, all seven of them that she could see. With all of them having the same characteristics of blond hair and green eyes, Elize instinctively knew who they were. Their recruitment and selection were a top-secret which she was not privy to. But she was aware of a project called 'Operation Sunset', which was said to be the last line of the defence programme. She did not know the details but looking at these young men moving up and down casually but alertly, she was reminded of the fervour of the Hitler Youth.

Elize recognised the look on their eyes – deadpan and tending to look far into the distance. They were dangerous and deliberately trained to be antisocial. No one knew of their existence, and the state didn't have any record of their lives. They lived completely off the grid.

And then an older man also appeared from the same shadows, and slowly but determinedly headed towards Elize's car. Determined not to let her own fear of these men show, Elize wound down her car's window, and greeted the approaching older man.

"Hi, my name is Martie Odendaal. Are you Captain Van Schalkwyk?" Elize asked.

"Yes, ma'am, Tiaan is my name," Tiaan said, extending his right hand. Elize noticed that he was tall, and well built, probably about 35 years old. His blond hair was crew cut and his face clean-shaven. He looked in fine physical shape, and Elize guessed that he either played tennis or was a swimmer. He was wearing green farm overalls and black hard boots, probably a part of camouflage, which would explain why he wanted to be called 'Tiaan' instead of 'Captain'.

Elize noted though that Tiaan did not introduce the others. Looking at them with their deadpan faces, Elize suspected that they would probably not welcome the introduction anyway.

"We've been expecting you. Everything is set. Come this way please," Tiaan said, continuing before Elize said anything else.

"Very well," Elize said curtly.

"Come this way then ma'am," Tiaan said, gesturing for Elize to get out of the car.

A few seconds later, Elize watched as Tiaan pulled open the large metal door of an adjacent sheep shearing shed, and as he switched on the high fluorescent lights. The bright light revealed several rows of what looked like supermarket shelves, fully stocked with what Elize immediately determined to be military weapons – thousands of assault rifles, rocket launchers, surface to air missiles, grenades of all kinds, thousands of handguns, boxes of munitions, fully laden machine gun bullet belts, magazines, the lot.

"This is out of inventory stock. There's a basement below, and there's more. We are ready," Said Tiaan, with a rather nonchalant tone of voice.

Elize did not reply. She had been aware for some time that there were stockpiles of weapons located at strategic depots all around the country, just in case the country was overrun and there was a need to quickly arm the white population. But she knew that in a situation where the exchange of power was negotiated, this place would have to be declared and handed over to the authorities. Otherwise, there was no other strategic significance to the armoury, except for distributing the weapons to the population, not when trouble starts, but ahead of it.

"Show me the other stuff," she ordered.

Tiaan understood the order, and he gestured for Elize to follow him to one corner of the shed where there was a strong safe door. After quickly punching a few numbers on a small electric pad on the side, the door made a whoosh sound as it sprang open.

The light was poor, giving a mysterious effect to the room. Elize noticed that Tiaan was suddenly quiet, only pointing and saying, "There it is."

Tiaan, of course, was pointing to what Elize later determined to be eight big metal boxes, more or less the size of an adult coffin. After looking the boxes over, as if to satisfy herself that everything was in order, she asked, "A truck was delivered here yesterday, right?"

"Yes, ma'am, it's at the back," Tiaan said.

"Good. Bring it about. These boxes must be loaded in it. The truck has a secret lower deck. Load them in there. When you are done, I'll tell you what to do next. Let's move," Elize said

Tiaan barked an order to the group of young men who were still sitting near the parking lot. In no time Elize heard the special purpose truck rumbling at the concrete front parkway of the farm. A while later, after Tiaan and his men were done loading the truck, exactly as directed by Elize, she called them aside and said, "You're leaving tonight. I suggest you lock up this place."

"Alright boss, where are we going to?" Tiaan asked.

"Port Elizabeth, near the harbour. I'll give the details of your contact there along the way. I want updates on everything that happens on the road. This truck must be protected all the way to Port Elizabeth," Elize said, and continued, handing Tiaan a card box full of walkie talkies, "We will communicate with each other through these two-way radios. They're secure."

"Yes ma'am, we have a discreet convoy of four cars, two behind and two in front of the truck. We also have a live tracking device in the truck. We will be fine," Tiaan said.

"Very well, I'll also be tagging along," Elize said, and continued to ask, "Is there a telephone here I can use? I need to call my hotel to tell them I won't be coming back tonight."

"Yes ma'am, this way," Tiaan said, showing Elize where the phone was.

Moments later, with Tiaan driving a double-cab Ford Ranger, and one of his young charges driving the truck, they left 'Farm 16', leaving the farm on remote lockdown.

***

At just after midnight, Tiaan's convoy passed the Karoo town of Beaufort West and proceeded on the N1 towards Aberdeen. Thus far, the journey had been pretty much free of incidents. The truck had only been briefly stopped by two traffic cops at Kleinpoort, and as it turned out, the two cops were very amenable to a handsome bribe.

However, as the convoy was approaching the town of Aberdeen, Tiaan radioed for Elize, saying, "Boss, there's a lot of strange static on our radio. I think someone is on to us."

"Can't be. I was assured these radios are clean," Elize said.

"It's not a foolproof thing, boss. I suggest we go silent for a while," Tiaan said.

"Roger that," Elize acknowledged.

Tiaan, of course, was correct. A Russian oil exploration company, which was ostensibly drilling for oil and doing fracking exploration in the Graaff-Reinet area, about 60 kilometres from Aberdeen, had picked up on their two-way communications. The company's name was RusOil Ltd. Its Director, Viktor Ustinov, together with two senior company executives, Vasily Popov and Abram Sokolov, were doing drilling operations around Graaff-Reinet in the Eastern Cape.

What no one knew though was that RusOil was a front for a Russian mafia operation. The Russians had become aware that South Africa's nuclear yield declared to the IAA was not complete, and that somewhere in South Africa, there existed someone who was in possession of weaponisable nuclear material, and they wanted to either buy the stuff or hijack it, preferably the latter.

At their offices in downtown Graaff-Reinet, they had set up what looked like ground testing equipment, but which in actual fact was the latest in area-wide listening technology, which could link up to any radio tower anywhere in South Africa. As Tiaan and his men were shepherding a cargo they knew little about, this group of Russian businesspeople were sitting at a bed and breakfast joint in Graaff-Reinet, with Viktor venting his frustrations at how slow everything was.

"Vasily, I'm bored. I can't take any more of this nonsense. I think it's time we cut our losses and return to Moscow. Really all this scouting of the drylands of the Eastern Cape, pretending like I'm interested in finding oil, whose hair-brained idea was this anyway?" Viktor asked, looking harassed.

"It was yours, boss, remember? You said for us to find the stuff, we must come to South Africa before things close, by which we took it you meant before the ANC comes to power," Vasily said.

"No man, I must have been mad. There is nothing here. After a year of looking, we must admit we were wrong. By the time I get back to Moscow, I will be cooked meat at this rate!" Viktor thundered.

"Well boss, maybe we're in luck," Vasily said, listening to a crackling sound from a two-way radio.

"What's up?" Viktor asked, suddenly his defeated demeanour changing.

"I've been listening to this chat for a while now. It's coming from a secure source, at least what they think is a secure source," Vasily said and continued before Viktor said anything else, "We've been tracking this for a while. It's on the road, just before Aberdeen. I think it's bound for Port Elizabeth."

"What are they saying?" Viktor asked.

"They keep saying stuff like, 'don't follow too close, keep trucking speed,'" Vasily said.

"Where do you think they're going?" Viktor asked.

"Looks like Port Elizabeth, but I can't say for sure," Vasily replied.

"OK," Viktor said and then continued, "get the GTi and go find out what's going on. Could be the stuff we've been looking for. Take Abram with you. Don't let them disappear into Port Elizabeth without finding out who they are."

***

The "discreet" convoy, as Tiaan called it, slowly snaked its way out of Klawer towards Vredendal and Calvinia via the R27, and onto the N1 highway towards Aberdeen. What Tiaan meant by "discreet" of course was that the truck would appear to be alone on the road, with all other support vehicles about a kilometre away from it. The idea was not to attract any attention to the truck, and that if such attention was attracted, the supporting vehicles would intervene, with extreme prejudice. This protocol would extend to both bona fide criminal hijackers, as well as inquisitive law enforcement.

At just after midnight, soon after passing the town of Graaff-Reinet, and headed in the direction of Port Elizabeth along the R75, about eighty kilometres away from Jansenville, Tiaan noticed a black Golf GTi that seemed to be interested in one of the cars in the convoy. The car had appeared out of nowhere at high speed and then slowed down about two hundred metres behind the second car. Tiaan observed the car for about five minutes trying to see if it would pass and disappear, or if it displayed any awareness of the full convoy, including the truck. He called on the driver of the car being followed by the Golf and asked him to rapidly increase speed. He wanted to see what the Golf's reaction would be, and sure enough, the Golf also rapidly increased its own speed to keep up.

To Tiaan, that behaviour immediately confirmed the Golf's tailing intention. He asked his driver to slow down to previous speed so that he is not too close to the truck. The Golf too slowed down. Thinking that they were getting close to making contact with their man at the PE harbour, and this would be a problem if it continued like this, Tiaan made another radio call to Elize.

"Boss, we have a tail. A black Golf GTi. What should we do?" He asked as soon as Elize picked up.

"Who do you think it is?" Elize asked.

"I don't know, but I've confirmed it," replied Tiaan.

"How many people are inside the car?" Elize asked.

"It looks like it's two, but I'm not sure," Tiaan replied.

"Alright, we can't have any screw-ups on this. I suggest you watch it for a while, and if it continues to threaten us, intercept, and terminate," Elize said, and continued, "and Tiaan, clean up immediately. The car and the bodies must not be found by the local cops. When you're done, drive to the town of Dispatch along the way and then stop and wait for me. There's a truck stop there near a garage. Wait there," Elize said, without hesitation.

"Roger that," said Tiaan, and then he relayed the order to his drivers, asking them to watch the GTI for a while. Not long afterwards, as the Golf GTi was passing a bushy area just after a small farming area known as Kuduskloof, Tiaan ordered his team to act, "Take the Golf out, now. Block and side swap it off the road, and terminate."

Immediately, two of Tiaan's cars sped up to the GTI, with the front car blocking it, while the one behind knocked it on its right back bumper, boxing it in and sending it on a tailspin off the road, and into the bushes. As the Golf was skidding out of control, the two cars that had blocked it pulled over on the kerb. The two drivers quickly alighted from the cars, with automatic rifles fitted with silencers at ready, and opened sustained fire at the Golf for about a minute and a half.

Tiaan later arrived on the scene and quickly verified that both driver and passenger in the Golf were dead, and noted that they were two white men, probably in their mid-forties. There was no form of identification on their bodies, and judging by the markings on the car, it was a rental. Looking at the time, Tiaan ordered everyone back into their cars, and they sped off to a rendezvous with Brigadier Elize Theron up Dispatch, about 15 kilometres away.

***

Meanwhile, as soon as she was done talking to Tiaan on the phone, Elize received a call from Dr Erasmus, saying, "We have a problem."

"Say that again! I was about to call you. We've just eliminated a tail," Elize said.

"I know," Dr Erasmus said.

"You know? Who were they?" Elize asked.

"People who wanted to hijack your cargo," Dr Erasmus said.

"What now? What's the problem?" Elize asked.

"Our friend at the harbour is pulling out of the deal. Poor chap, he's been spooked. You need to dump everything."

"Dump everything?!" Elize asked, almost screaming.

"Yep, think of something, fast. Whatever you do, that cargo must not reach the port. Send me the coordinates when done," Dr Erasmus said, and then the line went dead.

Elize cursed under her breath, and as the impact of the call from Dr Erasmus hit her, she cursed again out loud, "How the fuck do I dump eight coffin-sized boxes?!" But as Dr Erasmus had said, she had to think, fast. Almost instinctively, she increased the speed of her car, headed to her rendezvous with Tiaan at the garage at Dispatch.

***

"Who were those guys?" Tiaan asked as soon as he saw Elize alighting from her car.

"I'm not sure," Elize said, curtly.

"What does any of this mean?" Tiaan asked.

"It means we can no longer proceed to the harbour as planned. Our contact there has bailed," Elize said.

"Now what?" Tiaan asked.

"We have to dump the stuff," Elize said.

"What do you mean?" Tiaan asked, intrigued.

"I'd say we have about twenty-four hours before our cover is blown. It's daybreak now. We can't do anything during the day.

Let's wait here till dusk. In the meantime, we have to think what to do," Elize said.

"What do you have in mind, Boss?" Tiaan asked, resisting a temptation to ask what 'we' means in this context.

"Well, I've been thinking. You see these boxes already look like coffins. Why can't we bury them, just like coffins?" Elize asked, not necessarily directing the question to Tiaan.

"Really, where?" Tiaan asked, again resisting a strong temptation to tell Elize what he thought of her plan!

"I can't explain this now. Rather let's do this – leave the truck here with your boys. Let's take your bakkie and go to town. I'll tell you what my plan is," Elize said.

Still puzzled and sceptical, Tiaan forced himself to get into Elize's car. Moments later they were back on the N2, heading towards the Port Elizabeth city centre. On the way, they discussed the matter some more.

"OK, Tiaan, this is what I have in mind. My map says the nearest cemetery here is in Zwide Township. Let's go there now and check the place. My idea is that, from my experience, township graveyards are very busy, which means at any time there would be graves already dug up for the pending funerals," Elize said, matter of factly.

"But how do you know anything about graves in the townships?" Tiaan asked.

"Hello! Have you forgotten how long we've been in the townships – as the SADF I mean? Every weekend we've watched township funerals of activists. I've been to Avalon Cemetery in Soweto for instance. I've seen how they turn funerals into political rallies. More importantly for our purposes today, I know what it takes to organise a township funeral," Elize said.

"But you're overlooking one aspect. People. Hundreds of people being witnesses. What are you going to do about them? Besides, you can't just hijack other people's graves! Tell me you have a better plan than this!" Tiaan said, almost losing his sense of discipline about rank.

"That, my friend, is exactly what I propose to do, with your support of course," Elize said, emphatically.

"How?" Tiaan asked.

"Easy. We go to the cemetery. Buy the guards. Check the open graves. Extend the depth of the graves a little. Put the boxes in each extended grave. Put lintels above the boxes, so that there is something hard on top. Put the soil back up to the original depth of the grave, so that it looks like there is nothing beyond its normal depth. After that, we shall leave the grave open as the municipality left it," Elize said, without a hint of irony.

"You have money to buy the guards?" Tiaan asked.

"Yep. Plenty. As you know, in this country security guards are poorly paid. We shall show them a stack of cash. They will be impressed," Elize said.

"It's too risky!" Tiaan exclaimed.

"It will work," Elize said.

"But the guards, won't they talk?" Tiaan asked.

"They will. They don't have the training not to talk. This is too fascinating for them to resist not talking about it. So, we shall show them the money, give them the money, and then keep them with us the whole time, till we're done, and even use them as additional labour. When we're done, you will shoot them, and then we shall take their bodies with us as we leave, and dump them along the way," Elize said coldly.

"I see!" Tiaan exclaimed, looking at the Elize with searching eyes.

"Now, as soon as hardware stores open, I want us to buy picks, shovels and lintels. The size of the lintels must be 2 300 mm in length and must cover the grave width of 900 mm. The normal depth of a grave in South Africa is 2 000 mm. I want us to extend this by a further 1 000 mm," Elize said.

"Boss, somehow I don't want to know how you know all this!" Tiaan again exclaimed.

About thirty minutes after they'd left the truck stop near a garage at Dispatch, Tiaan's bakkie arrived at the Zwide Cemetery and paused for a moment not far from the main gate. The time was now at just after seven in the morning. The sky was clear, and it was already warm, giving a clear indication that this was going to be a very hot day.

Elize and Tiaan got out of the car and wandered towards the guardhouse which was about fifty metres from where they'd parked. When they arrived at the guardhouse, they found two guards, who seemed to be preparing to go home, as they were busy collecting and packing their things in their backpack bags.

"Hi guys, how are you?" Elize asked, suddenly aware that it might look odd to these guards to be receiving two white visitors so bloody early in the morning!

"My name is Brigadier Theron, and this is Captain Schalkwyk," Elize said, without waiting for a reply, and very deliberately using formal police ranks.

One of the guards replied, "*Molo* madam. My name is Nceba, and this here is my colleague Mzubanzi. What can we do for you?"

"You work night shift?" Elize asked.

"Yes, ma'am. It's already *tshayile* time, but our truck is late," Nceba said.

"Oh, I see. So, you will be back here tonight?" Elize asked.

"*Ewe*, Madam," Nceba replied.

"Very well then, we will see you tonight. We are checking this place up. There's going to be a funeral of a gangster here in the next twenty-four hours. We don't want anyone shooting guns in the air," Elize said, again deliberately making reference to gangster funerals which she knew these guards would relate to.

"Ah yes ma'am, those ones can be a real nuisance!" Mzubanzi said, speaking for the first time.

"Good then. We will be here tonight just to prepare things. Do you mind if we check the cemetery up a bit?" Elize said.

"No problem, ma'am," Nceba said.

A while later, Elize and Tiaan were slowly strolling along the narrow aisles among the cemetery graves and were satisfied with what they found – about fifteen open graves that were scheduled to be used in the next twenty-four hours. And then they came back to Nceba and Mzubanzi, with a proposition.

"By the way, you work alone most of the time? I mean there are no other people, say from the municipality that check this place at night, right?" Elize asked.

"Yes, madam, we work alone here. Why do you ask?" Mzubanzi asked.

"Well, I have something here for you," Elize said and continued before either of the two security guards could ask further questions, "you see my friend is carrying a suitcase. It has money, two hundred thousand rand in all, and it's yours." As she pointed to the suitcase, Elize gestured to Tiaan to open it, and said, "You can count it if you like."

Both Mzubanzi and Nceba gawked and whistled at the sight of so much money. Shaking his head in amazement, Nceba said, "No madam, we will count it later! Now what? What do you want from us?"

"It's simple. You see those open graves there?" Elize asked.

"Yes ma'am, they're for tomorrow's funerals," Mzubanzi said, looking puzzled.

"Each of those graves is about two metres deep, right?" Elize asked.

"Yes, madam, I guess. Why?" Nceba asked, clearly puzzled at this line of questioning.

"Tonight, I want you to more or less double that," Elize said.

"You want us to what?" Mzubanzi asked, his voice becoming a high-pitched whisper.

"You heard me. I want you to make those holes about four metres deep," Elize said.

"But why?" Nceba and Mzubanzi asked, almost at the same time.

"The bag I've just given you is the reason you're not supposed to question my reasons. If you want the money, just do what I ask, nothing more nothing less," Elize said, with a certain finality in her tone.

"Alright, I guess it's none of our business. What else do you want us to do?" Nceba asked, keen not to lose this manna from heaven!

"As I was saying, each of the graves that have already been dug for the coming funerals, I want you to make them four metres deep. In other words, as they are already two metres, I want you to dig a further two metres. I want a double-decker arrangement, such that when the mourners arrive, they must not see that the grave is deeper than usual," Elize said.

"So, let me see if I get this – we dig, let you bury something, and then cover the grave up to the normal depth?" Nceba asked, sounding excited.

"Exactly. And another thing, you are not going to go home just yet. Right now, you are coming with us to town now, where we will all buy the necessary tools for this job," Elize said.

"I see! Hey but it's OK," Mzubanzi declared.

"We are going to be together the whole day today. Take all your things and put them in the boot of my car. We shall start the job tonight, just as soon as your night shift starts. Now let's move. Your day shift guys are almost here. Don't say a word of this to them, unless you don't mind splitting your money with them," Elize said, sternly.

"What? No ways!" Nceba swore.

Later that evening, Elize, Tiaan, Nceba and Mzubanzi, followed by what Nceba thought was a scary truck, started digging the already dug graves at Zwide Cemetery.

TEN YEARS LATER,
WINTER OF 2000

Project Echo is a Go

On Tuesday, the 6th of June 2000, retired Major General Jan Kloppers was celebrating the 21st birthday of his granddaughter, Suzette Marais-Kloppers, at his farm at Schweizer-Reneke in the North West Province. It was a big event. The Kloppers had decided to spare no expense, and invitations were sent to all friends and relatives from all over the country to partake in the celebration, and they had obliged.

Even though the celebrations were set to start at ten o'clock in the evening, by about eight o'clock the farm was already buzzing with inebriated partygoers, who had gathered around a big spitfire braai. The party, of course, was set to be an all-night affair, with live performances from some of the country's top Afrikaans musicians. A big stage was constructed in the vast premises of the farm, and by ten o'clock, the revelry had gathered full steam.

What of course no one knew was that General Kloppers had a double motive for organising this event. He also wanted a plausible reason for getting all his other friends under one roof, for a special meeting. He was using the event as a cover for an important meeting of members of Project Echo.

In the consolidated list of invites, which he and Suzette spent time compiling, General Kloppers included people such as Professor Marlon Hendricks, Professor Aidan van Heerden, who came all the way from Australia and was due to go back the following evening, Lieutenant Colonel Hein Terblanche, Lieutenant Colonel Andy Malan, Mncedisi Mmango and sixteen other people.

General Kloppers insisted that among the many chalets on his farm, one must be prepared for his friends alone. As the party was starting in earnest, with General Kloppers expected to grace it and make a speech, he decided to first meet with his friends in the designated chalet.

With drinks flowing generously to everyone in the room, General Kloppers called everyone to order, saying, "Ladies and Gentlemen, I called you here to tell you that Project Echo has reached maturity. At 12 noon on the 15th of July 2000, down in Port Elizabeth, earth shall breathe fire. To our friends, led here by my brother the Minister of Defence, Mr Mncedisi Mmango, I have taken the liberty of purchasing tickets to various destinations around the world, to facilitate your absence from the events that will unfold on the 15th of July. I will call you later that day and recite our mantra, and you'll take that as a command to come back and assume leadership of the situation as would have developed at that point. In the meantime, I have also decided to reward all of you for staying the course with Project Echo. So if you will all be so kind and give me the keys to your cars, I'll see to it that my people put presents in the boots of each of your cars. I might add, each present is worth three million rand. That is all that I wanted to say, and I strongly suggest that we do not discuss anything about what I've just said. In short, Project Echo is a go, and you all know the applicable protocols. Now ladies and gentlemen, let us celebrate my granddaughter's birthday."

With that, all who were in the room quietly filed out, with most of them headed to their cars to check out these promised 'presents'. And sure enough, as the party was in full swing, the recipients of General Klopper's largesse were on cloud nine, because as it turned out, their presents were in fact boxes filled with gold bars.

The Hit on Martie Odendaal

It was the afternoon of Sunday the 11th of June 2000, and Cynthia was listening to this *"Somagwaza"* song coming out of the bushes in front of her house for the umpteenth time. She could just about eat her own head! The worse thing was that each time the men sang this song, some among them would yell at her to go back inside the house, while others would just flash her. She had had enough of being treated like the enemy of whatever kind of regressive progress this was, of being held prisoner in her own house, and of being subjected to a macabre show every June or December!

"Seriously we must move! I really can't deal with this!" said Cynthia, looking accusingly at her husband.

"What are you talking about?" asked Phila, looking perplexed and dumbfounded by this sudden and out of context outburst.

"I'm talking about all these fires they're making at that initiation camp. It's the fourth one now, and all the smell is coming straight to my house! Exactly what are they burning?" Cynthia replied, seething.

"They're burning what they're burning, none of which concerns you, woman! You want me to talk to you about what men do in the bush now? Women today! Next, you gonna want to be the bush doctor yourself!" Phila replied, with exaggerated sarcasm.

"*Ag*, I'd probably do a better job than the bunch of you! Anyway, my concern is being subjected to the smells of burning bomas, every blessed day in all the Junes of the year! I want us to move to a new house!" Cynthia replied in a similar acerbic tone.

"We can't just up and move to another place just because of an initiation season!" Phila replied exasperatedly.

"You can stay if you like! Me, I can't be sniffing initiates medicine every day. Come to think of it! No wonder I've been having bad dreams lately! I'm gonna leave you here if you don't want us to move. Besides, we have another problem," Cynthia said emphatically.

"Another problem? Like what?" Phila asked, curious.

"Honey, have you ever thought that maybe the folks next door are dangerous killers – you know, serial killers, assassins and whatnot?" Cynthia asked, without a tinge of cynicism in her voice.

"And they have not killed us yet, after fifteen years of being their neighbours, because . . .?" Phila said, with contrived disbelief.

"I don't know, maybe we've not done anything yet that offends them," Cynthia said, feeling somewhat chastised by her husband's mocking tone.

"But if they hear you asking about them now, they may kill us for sure! What's your concern about them anyway?" Phila asked.

"I was just thinking about your sermon at church today. I mean, how can you love thy neighbour if you don't even know them?" Cynthia asked

"Are you saying my sermon was hypocritical?" Phila asked, feeling his turn at being chastised.

"A tad yes!" Cynthia said.

"Aren't you abusing your proximity to the priest?" Phila asked.

"I sleep with this priest! Besides, you're not really a priest. You're a church elder," Cynthia said, laughing.

"Hey if I act on behalf of the priest, then I'm a priest at that moment!" Phila said, he too laughing.

"Still, you're not supposed to say things you yourself don't believe in!" Cynthia said.

"Why are you in such a tempter today? Soon you'll be bringing me stones to test if I can turn them into bread!" Phila said, and continued, "but, back to your question, what strikes me is how anyone can drive a three million-rand Porsche and then live in a half a million rand house!"

"That's what strikes you? Not that there's not been a sound of a child coming from that house? Not that we have not heard any kind of human conversation? Have you ever seen our neighbour's washing hanging on the line? Or for that matter the neighbour himself? All we see every day is a big car with heavily tinted windows coming in and out of the house. For all we know it could be driven by an alien!" Cynthia said excitedly.

The conversation went on, back and forth for some time. They were, of course, talking about the house at 14 Curtis Road in Amalinda, East London, which always seemed deserted. Only at night, when the lights would be switched on, would it be apparent that there was someone in it. The other sign of life was how immaculate everything about it always looked. The sidewalk lawn was trimmed and cut every Tuesday. The red roof tiles looked freshly painted at all times. The tall perimeter wall was also very neat, with an aluminium gate that was always closed, and with a poster that showed a foreboding picture of a pit bull.

Phila had to concede that his wife was correct. For as long as he'd lived on this street, he had never seen or even heard the voices of his neighbours. Sometimes, on days when he would come home late at night drunk, he would call out over their dividing fence, '*makhelwane!*' But there would be no response. At some point, Phila began to lose interest in the identity of his neighbour. Besides, he figured, it was a fashionable thing in this new South Africa for neighbours not to know each other. Much as he would have preferred to be an exception in this regard, he began to accept that he too was in the statistic that didn't know their neighbours.

Today, thanks to prodding by his wife, he revisited the matter in his head. He had never thought that anything was sinister about their neighbour, just that he was reclusive, that's all. But he had to admit that Cynthia, ever with a fertile imagination, was on to something. Was this guy a serial killer or what? And if he was, what was he, a lowly acting priest, to do about it? It's not as if he could walk up to him, place the hand of God on his head and pray that he ceases and desists with his sinning ways!

But knowing his wife, Phila knew that she would not let this matter go unless and until he'd gone over to this strange neighbour's house and find out more about him. She was like a pit bull his wife, Phila thought wryly. He would go and meet his neighbour, he decided.

The time was just after seven in the evening. The neighbour's light was on, and Phila took that as the cue for him to go and press the neighbour's gate buzzer. But as he left his front entrance, something checked his movement. He froze in midstride and quickly scanned his surroundings. Other than the usual street light poles, one of which had a flashing lightbulb, he didn't see anything. Yet he knew he'd seen a silhouette of something or someone crouched just outside his gate.

Phila didn't have to wonder long. At first, it sounded like crickets. In June though? Phila wondered. It couldn't be. Now fully aware and suddenly realising that this was the sound of a semi-automatic rifle, right next to his house! He heard voices, people speaking rapidly, whispering loudly, and cursing crudely – all in Afrikaans. He heard screams, more particularly the scream of a woman, and the screeching sound of a motor vehicle speeding away. And then there was silence. Whatever it was, it was over.

Cynthia, who had been busy cooking in the kitchen, also came outside after hearing the gunshots and was visibly relieved to see that it was not her husband to whom these shots were targeted.

"What is happening?" Cynthia asked, sounding concerned.

"I have no idea, let's call the police," Phila said, quickly scrolling through his cell phone for police numbers.

When the police came about twenty minutes later, Phila was on hand to show them his neighbour's house. The police vehicle was quickly followed by a police pathology vehicle, as well as a police forensics van. Phila noticed that the police had not called for an ambulance and figured the pathology vehicle suggested that someone at his neighbour's house had died.

A while later, about thirty minutes since they'd come, the police finally came out of the house, headed to their vehicles. Phila, curious to know what had happened, asked one of the officers as they passed him on their way to their cars, "Who died?"

"The owner of the house, Ms Martie Odendaal," came the curt reply from the officer.

On the Scent of the Scoundrels

On the 18th of June 2000, a week after the death of Brigadier Elize Theron under a mysterious hail of bullets, news broke that the last Director-General of apartheid civilian intelligence-gathering organisation, the NIS, 76-year-old Dr Hans Erasmus, had died in hospital after a long and unknown illness. The Afrikaans newspaper *Rapport* was screaming the news in its headline *"Hoe Erasmus gesterf het"*. The *Pretoria News* was also doing the same with its headline *"All apartheid secrets gone"*, which was blazoned on lamp posts all over the capital city.

The current Director-General of State Security Agency, Dr Loraine Nceka, was slightly bemused as she made her way into Dr Erasmus's Waterkloof house to pay her respects. It seemed strange that someone who spent his entire life in the shadows was receiving this much publicity.

But Dr Nceka quickly cast the lamp post images aside. She had important business to attend to. She was on her way to pay her respects to Mrs Anna Marie Erasmus, the widow of Dr Erasmus. However, besides the human element of her visit, she had an even more important objective. Protocol required that if a senior intelligence officer dies, regardless of how long they'd been out of service, the state must take custody of all their possessions, including papers, computer hard drives, cell phones, books, manuscripts etc., to determine any aspects of such that may be part of national security. These, of course, would all be returned unless they are determined to be of national interest.

Dr Nceka was coming to Dr Erasmus's house to perform this duty. She was quite aware of the intrusive nature of the task, which is why she was doing it herself, instead of delegating it to one of her DDG's.

As soon as she arrived, accompanied by two young cadets from her Registry Division, Dr Nceka introduced herself to Mrs Erasmus, the grieving wife of Dr Erasmus, in Afrikaans laden with a thick Xhosa accent, "*Goeiemore, Tannie. Hoe gaan dit?* My name is Dr Loraine Nceka. I'm the DG of State Security," she said.

"*Oh, ag baie dankie,* Dr Nceka. I've heard so much about you from my husband. Indeed your reputation precedes you," Mrs Erasmus said.

Dr Nceka, of course, knew that even though Mrs Erasmus was not an intelligence functionary, there were files in the office which suggested that she'd offered more than a helping hand to her husband on matters of intelligence.

"I'm sorry for your loss, *Tannie.* Please accept the condolences of government," Dr Nceka said.

"Thank you, Dr Nceka. It means a lot. My husband had been seriously ill for quite some time. We are sad for his passing, but we're relieved that he is not in pain anymore. Thank you for coming. And just so you know, I'm aware that my husband's things must be handed over to the state for security verification. If you want to do that now, you're more than welcome," Mrs Erasmus said.

Dr Nceka was quite pleased to find that she would not have to press Mrs Erasmus for the personal effects of her husband. She replied, "Thank you, *Tannie.* I'm glad for your understanding. As you know, these matters are required to be dispensed with as soon as humanly possible. Therefore yes, I would like to do that now."

"Very well. Just take what you need. Know this, though, I'm giving you my husband's things in good faith. This is not permission to besmirch my husband's name in any shape or form," Mrs Erasmus said sternly.

"I give you my word, *Tannie*, there are no malicious intentions behind my request," Dr Nceka said.

Mrs Erasmus nodded her head, and said, "In that case, come this way. All my husband's papers are in the study, in the basement."

When they arrived at the study, Mrs Erasmus opened the door, and then said, "There Doc, I'll leave you alone."

"Once again, thank you, *Tannie*," Dr Nceka said, as she gestured to the two young men accompanying her to look around the study. They were carrying clipboards with a list of items to look for.

From that moment on, Dr Nceka was allowed to quietly and unobtrusively take what she needed from the house of Dr Hans Erasmus. About an hour later, she and her team left with a number of boxes containing all the intelligence value items. Dr Nceka was determined to quickly process the stuff and either return it as soon as possible or quickly communicate her intentions about it to Mrs Erasmus.

***

Later that afternoon, at about five o'clock, Dr Nceka was back at her office at the Musanda Complex at Delmas Road, Greenstone, in Pretoria. Situated in a corner on the tenth floor, her office was vast, measuring more than 300 square foot, and sparsely furnished. There was a big imbuia wood desk facing the city skyline in the distance. In the centre of the office, there was a large conference table, which could seat ten people, and there was only one item on top of it, a red landline phone.

Dr Loraine Nceka, commonly referred to by her clan name "MamCethe" by her peers, was a stout and busty 56-year-old woman, with a strong and coarse voice. When she laughs, her whole body would shake, and when she's angry or giving a stern directive, the coarse texture of her voice would turn raspy and uncompromising. Her long and black dyed hair was always pushed back and tied into a ponytail. With her dimpled and bespectacled face, she tended to have an officious and matronly look, which was complemented by a disarming smile.

Staff members at the Musanda Complex just referred to her as "Boss Lady" or plainly "Boss". Today everybody in the building could see that the Boss Lady was in a sort of serious mood. Everybody knew that if you bumped into her in the lift, and she was not in a conversational mood, she had a way of conveying this without uttering a single word. Anyone calling her office for an appointment would first ask if her sentences were short or long that day because they knew that if she explains herself when giving an instruction, then she's in a good mood. If she uses single word replies to complex matters, then you know you must come back some other time.

As she settled in her office desk, and her body quickly getting used to the contrast of the cold outside and the warmth of her office, Dr Nceka readied herself for the task of going through the material from Dr Erasmus's estate. She took off her long black coat, revealing her black pleated skirt and a short-sleeved linen blouse.

In no time after that, Dr Nceka was engrossed in files covering an era she only read about from some of the old spooks at Musanda Complex. Even when her PA, the lovely Dimpho Malindi, just budged in without knocking, her eyes didn't move an inch from the papers. Dimpho instinctively knew that she must retreat. She wanted to talk to her boss about her diary for the following day. But when she saw the look on Dr Nceka's face,

Dimpho felt it could wait. Even as she was usually casual in her interactions with her boss, Dimpho knew her enough to know when disturbances were not welcome.

As Dimpho was tiptoeing out of the room, trying to gently close the door behind her, Dr Nceka called her, "Er Dimps, I think you can go home now. I'm pulling an all-nighter tonight."

"Oh really, thanks ma'am," Dimpho said excitedly.

"Keep your phone open though," Dr Nceka said.

"Will do ma'am, thanks again," Dimpho said and walked out of the room.

With Dimpho gone and most of her staff in units adjacent to her office also gone for the day, Dr Nceka lined up Dr Erasmus' boxes on her conference table. The first box had a stack of what looked like academic papers, essays in a range of subjects.

Soon after that, thanks to the organised manner of the material, Dr Nceka quickly ascertained that these were mostly position papers Dr Erasmus had drawn up to assist the National Party's negotiations effort during the 1990s CODESA negotiations. They included concepts for the new structure of post-apartheid intelligence; suggestions on how the military organisations of the ANC, PAC and the homelands should be integrated with the SADF; suggestions on how the new police force should be structured; some thoughts on safeguarding minority group rights; opinions on the workability of the far-right's notion of a *volkstaat*; a critique of the ANC's insistence on mass struggle during negotiations; some thoughts on electoral systems in a context where there was a huge majority black electorate alongside a minuscule minority white group; and a strategic perspective on the pros and cons of the violence that was raging in many townships in the Reef.

Dr Nceka quietly read all this with growing fascination. The papers took her back to a time she regarded as most interesting in the country's history, which saw truly hurly-burly moments such as the unbanning of political organisations, the release of political prisoners, including the release of Nelson Mandela, the negotiations for a democratic South Africa, the assassination of Chris Hani, wanton state-sponsored violence, counter mobilisation by the right wing, the first inclusive national election of the 27th of April 1994, and the inauguration of Nelson Mandela as the first black President of a democratic South Africa.

Dr Nceka had never actually thought about the 'regime's side of things except that they needed to fall, and let Mandela take over! At the time when these great changes were happening in the country, she'd been a forty-two-year-old academic at the University of Transkei, teaching Political Science.

But Dr Nceka quickly reminded herself that her mission today was not the fascination she felt, but national security. The reason she was reading this stuff was to determine its security relevance, not a joyride along memory lane!

Having made her mind that these papers were not relevant for her present purposes, she made a note which she would send to Mrs Erasmus asking her to donate the papers to a university – that is if there were no plans to establish a foundation in memory of Dr Erasmus.

And then she grabbed another box and pried it open. Immediately her mood changed, from fascination to mild irritation and curiosity. There were different kinds of papers in this one, she soon noted, all of which concerned South Africa's nuclear development programme. This was strange, she thought. As far as she knew, all material relating to the Pelindaba Project was deposited *holus-bolus* to the International Atomic Agency years ago. The terms of the closure of the program were that there would not be anyone in possession of any material relating to how the apartheid state made nuclear weapons, least of all a private individual.

With her interest more than piqued, Dr Nceka flipped the whole box over and spread the papers across the full length of the table, determined not to miss a single thing. There was a range of items, which she started to rearrange according to their themes. There were a number of documents which were specifically focused on the inspection of the country's nuclear programme sometime in 1990, soon after the FW de Klerk speech.

In the main, these documents were describing the facility of Pelindaba, the yield of uranium and plutonium found on site, the number of fully developed nuclear devices the South African state was able to manufacture, the IAA's overall satisfaction that government had collaborated well in the effort to end the nuclear programme, and the IAA's confirmation that South Africa had successfully developed six nuclear bombs.

Still irritated that she should read about this stuff from the personal collection of her predecessor, Dr Nceka's attention was drawn to a piece of paper which appeared to be an unmarked addendum to the main report, with the following rather cryptic note:

"The amount of plutonium found by the IAA is not consistent with the previously reported yield. There was no account given on what happened to an amount of plutonium from which three nuclear bombs could plausibly be made. However, the IAA considered the disclosure of the previous National Party government to be in good faith and accepted the explanation that the yield was possibly over-estimated from the beginning. The pressure to conclude this work before the ANC takeover contributed to the abandoning of any attempts to establish the full extent of this matter. The yield unaccounted for is available and ready for weaponization."

"Huh?!" Dr Nceka heard her own scream after reading this note. Available, how? she asked herself, of course getting none the wiser. Now feeling hot under the collar, she went through the rest of the documents in the box, almost rummaging through the stuff, and found a list of the names of physicists who worked on South Africa's nuclear programme before it was closed.

There were eight names, two of whom were redacted.

Seeing the blocked-out spaces, Dr Nceka sighed heavily and scratched her head. As far as she was concerned, the names of physicists who are working on a nuclear development program are by default top-secret, and this applies to all of them equally. Why then have a list which reveals the majority of them but hides two of them? She didn't have an answer to this question.

She put the matter aside for now and decided to call Vumile Menzeni, one of her deputies.

"Quick question. How do I unredact a name?" Dr Nceka asked, as soon as Vumile answered.

"Is there even such a word in English?" Vumile asked, laughing.

"Mr Menzeni, this is a serious enquiry!" Dr Nceka said admonishingly.

"Sorry, Boss. Well, can I send somebody over to you rather than me explaining it to you?" Vumile asked.

"Yep, do that, now if you can, please," Dr Nceka said, curtly.

"Sure, Luca Verster from Forensics will be there just now," Vumile said.

"Good," Dr Nceka said and cut the call.

After that, she proceeded to make herself a cup of coffee. This was going to be a long night, she thought. Her mind wandered back to Dr Erasmus, asking, what was this man up to?

A few minutes later, Luca Verster, the head of the Forensics and Signals division, walked in at Dr Nceka's office, carrying a black briefcase.

"Oh good, you're here. Help me with this, will you?" Dr Nceka said, skipping the pleasantries.

"Alright, Boss, let's see," Luca said, taking the blocked-out document from Dr Nceka's hand. He took one look at it and then opened his briefcase and took out what looked to Dr Nceka like a document scanner, albeit more sophisticated.

Dr Nceka, of course, knew that the agency did have the capacity to reverse or un-erase obscured information. She'd seen and approved the strategic inventory list of the SSA but had never seen the equipment up close. She watched with fascination as Luca took the list from her and put it through a horizontal crevice on the one end of the machine, and as it buzzed in, quite like a fax machine. Seconds later, the document emerged from the other side of the machine, magically revealing the two names that had been obscured.

"There you're Boss. I'll leave you now if that's ok with you," said Luca, disrupting Dr Nceka's fascination.

"Wait, Luca, there's something else. I found this calculator here. At least I think it's a calculator. I find it strange though that it should be buried here, and it's not the usual brand – you know, such as your Casio, HP, Hitachi, Sharp, Sanyo," Dr Nceka said, handing Luca the 'calculator'.

Luca took one look, pried the device open at the back, and said, "Ma'am this is not a calculator. This thing's circuitry is more complex than a calculator's. Let me take it to our lab. I'll tell you within the next hour what it is."

"Fine, but please bring it back," Dr Nceka said sternly.

As Luca was going out of the door, Dr Nceka looked at the two names coming out of Luca's machine. These were two names of people she'd never heard of before, not that she knew any nuclear physicists. But in her line work, she had a general idea of who was who in most fields of strategic security importance. The names were Professors Aidan van Heerden and

Marlon Hendricks, both nuclear physicists previously with the University of Stellenbosch, at least from what she could glean from a quick google search.

She decided to call Vumile again, "Man, something else, I need to urgently find out where Professors Aidan van Heerden and Marlon Hendricks are at the moment. They were previously on the staff establishment of the Pelindaba project in the 80s. Do a quiet check, will you?"

"What's up, Boss?" Vumile asked, curious.

"I don't know ... yet. Have a feeling about it, though. Get back to me pronto, will you?" Dr Nceka said and dropped the line.

Dr Nceka sighed and moved to the next box with Dr Erasmus's personal effects. This one contained a stack of what appeared to be random papers. Her curiosity was drawn though to a handwritten note. It was just a piece of paper, the kind a person hurriedly grabs to jot down a telephone message, and on it, there were numbers – place coordinates to be exact. Dr Nceka called Luca again and asked him to check what these were coordinates of.

* * *

Moments later, Luca called back, saying, "Boss, that calculator thing of yours is actually a very powerful custom-made remote control. The buttons are fake. They're not connected to the circuitry. This is the kind of thing you wire yourself when you want to use it. I don't know what it controls, but not to be alarmist or anything, I'd say there is a very powerful explosive device at the end of this."

"Thank you, Luca. And those coordinates?" Dr Nceka asked.

"It's the damnedest thing! They show a cemetery in Port Elizabeth, Zwide Cemetery," Luca said.

"A cemetery in a township! I see! Thanks again, Luca. That'll be all," Dr Nceka said and dropped the line.

Dr Nceka had still not gone through all the Erasmus material by 10 o'clock in the evening. With everybody now long gone, the building was eerily quiet. The only sounds she could hear were those of cars rumbling and hooting down in the street, as well as the wheezing and howling of winter winds, which added to a rather spooky ambience.

Even though Dr Nceka was not done yet, and still unsure of what to make of Dr Erasmus's papers, a disturbing picture had begun to emerge. Not wanting to jump to any premature conclusions about anything, she decided to call the national Commissioner of Police, General Andrew Moss, not to report a crime per se, but to seek the counsel of someone she implicitly trusted.

"General, sorry to call you so late," Dr Nceka said as soon as her call was picked up by the Commissioner.

"MamCethe, I don't believe that you're sorry. Otherwise, you would not do something you're sorry for! Only criminals do that! What can I do for you?" the Commissioner asked, with a distinct touch of humour in his voice.

"I'll go straight to it. General, I need your help, urgently," Dr Nceka began to say.

"Listen, I don't deal with ghosts. Call me if there's a murderer I need to arrest!" the Commissioner thundered over the phone.

"I know, I know, hear me out will you! As you know in the 90s, I was an academic, far away from the daily grind of ANC politics. I need to speak to someone who was in charge of ANC intelligence in the 90s," Dr Nceka said.

"I see! Well the former President of the ANC would be one such person," the Commissioner said, chuckling.

"No. He's too political. I need someone with operational knowledge, someone who was keeping tabs on what the apartheid intelligence apparatus was doing when the political negotiations were happening," Dr Nceka said.

"Alright, I see what you mean. I'll send you the number of someone I know. She's retired now but is still doing freelance, just in case you want to use her. Her name is Miranda Milile – one very tough cookie. I need to know though, where are you headed with this?" the Commissioner asked.

"For now, I don't know. But going through Dr Erasmus's personal effects, I'm left with a nasty feeling that our unresolved past may be just about to catch up with us rather spectacularly," Dr Nceka reply.

"Keep me posted Loraine. I hate not knowing!" the Commissioner said.

"Indeed, indeed. As soon as I know anything for sure. You will be the first to know," Dr Nceka said.

"Now, as I say, her name is Miranda Milile. She was running most of the ANC's sensitive security operations. I'll ask Luthuli House for her number," the Commissioner said and ended the call.

A short while later, Dr Nceka received the contact details of Ms Miranda Milile via SMS, and she made a mental note of calling this number as soon as she was done going through Dr Erasmus's boxes.

The next box she looked at was no less astounding. Even though she didn't know what to expect in this box, she was shocked at what she found. There was nothing much in it except for a black file, which contained the operational record of one Brigadier Elize Theron, including pictures of people she had killed in combat, people she kidnapped and tortured and later killed, as well as maps and directions to where they were buried in unmarked graves, both inside the country and in northern Namibia and southern Angola.

With her suspicions now all but confirmed, at about twelve o'clock midnight, Dr Nceka finally finished processing the Erasmus material. She remembered the promise she made to Mrs Erasmus, that the , would not be used in a manner that besmirches her husband's name. But now that she had seen Dr Erasmus's papers, keeping this promise would be a hard sell, she thought, with a heavy sigh.

But she was still not ready to go home and sleep just yet. There were still a number of loose ends she wanted to be tied up. She decided to call Dimpho, her PA, "Dimps, I'm an educated woman. I can tell time. So please don't give me a time question-and-answer test! And I know I said you could go home, but I never said I would not call you."

With Dimpho chuckling in the background, Dr Nceka continued, "Something has come up. As soon as you come in, in the morning, I need you to cancel all my engagements tomorrow, please."

"Yes ma'am, will do," Dimpho said.

Soon after calling Dimpho, Dr Nceka received a call from Vumile, saying, "Boss, about the list you gave me; I've just sent you an email on that, and other related matters."

"Thank you. And Vumile, I need something else. I need the name of someone I can ask to work on a special project for me. Someone outside the agency," said Dr Nceka.

"A researcher?" Vumile asked.

"No, a special ops person," Dr Nceka said.

"Alright, Boss, I hear you. I'll send a file through in the morning," Vumile said.

Soon after ending the call from Vumile, Dr Nceka quickly opened her computer and read Vumile's email with growing alarm. When she was done reading the email, she put the computer aside, promising herself to return to it later.

At about twenty minutes past midnight, Dr Nceka placed a call to Ms Miranda Milile. She had a mischievous expression on her face as she listened to the phone ringing about eight times before Miranda picked up. She was not surprised by the surly tone of Miranda's voice and the fact that Miranda didn't say the usual 'hello'. She just yelled, "Really! At this hour? Whoever you are this better be good!"

Dr Nceka decided to be very formal in her approach, figuring this would give Miranda a moment of pause. "Ms Milile," she said, "my name is Dr Loraine Nceka. I'm the Director-General of the State Security Agency. I received your number from the National Commissioner of Police, General Andrew Moss."

Dr Nceka could hear Miranda calming herself down. Of course, Miranda was very aware who Dr Nceka was, and instinctively she sat up from her bed, fully expecting this to be neither a prank nor a social call, before asking, "Hello Dr Nceka, what can I do for you?"

"Firstly, please accept my apology for calling you at this hour. I would have called you in the morning if it was possible, but matters of state don't keep to our human rhythms," Dr Nceka said.

"Indeed, ma'am. I too apologise for how I reacted to this call. It's been a while since I've stayed awake waiting and making calls at any damn time I please. I've forgotten how it's like. Still, you have me curious," Miranda said, with a suppressed chuckle.

It was an infectious chuckle, as Dr Nceka laughed just before saying, "Just a quick question then. Did the ANC ever investigate the apartheid-era nuclear program?"

"We did actually, albeit briefly," Miranda asked, wondering and scratching her head.

"Why briefly, if I may ask?" Dr Nceka asked.

"Well, as you can imagine, there were more urgent things at the time. The re-entry of the ANC leadership into the country, the township violence, and the military integration process – all those were uppermost in our minds. The regime was also burning all incriminating evidence of torture and death squads, and we wanted to save as much of this as possible. The nuclear capacity of the apartheid state was something we needed time to study first before we could do anything meaningful about, which we didn't have. Once the IAA issued its report declaring the program effectively neutered, that also signalled the end of our interest in the matter," Miranda said, still puzzling about why the DG of SSA was digging up apartheid files.

"And the little that you did? What did it focus on?" Dr Nceka asked.

"We were concerned about the security of the program. It was interesting, actually. Just as we were concerned about apartheid leaders selling nuclear secrets to their friends in the West, apartheid and its friends were concerned about our friendship with Fidel Castro, Muammar Gaddafi, and Mugabe! In fact, it was our view at the time that if we showed much interest in the nuclear programme, the CIA and others might work to scupper the negotiations rather than risk these weapons falling into the hands of what they called 'rogue states'. When we lost interest in the matter we were pursuing an Israeli connection, and even though we never could prove it, we were convinced that De Klerk had a plan B in the event the negotiations fail, which involved either the Israeli state or rogue elements within it," Miranda said.

"Any particular name you were pursuing?" Dr Nceka asked.

"There was one arms merchant – a former SADF Lieutenant Colonel Hein Terblanche, who also went by an assumed name of Peter Weir. He vanished into thin air. But as I say, the ANC lost interest in the matter altogether," Miranda said.

"Alright, thank you, Miranda, you've been more than helpful. I don't suppose I need to remind you that this conversation is classified, do I?" Dr Nceka asked.

"No, ma'am, I understand perfectly, and I must say you have me curious," Miranda said.

"You know better than most Ms Milile, curiosity killed the cat. Let's do lunch some time," Dr Nceka said, ominously, and ended the call.

When Dr Nceka was done talking to Miranda, the time was just after one o'clock in the morning. "I'm done," she whispered to herself. She put everything back inside the boxes. In the morning she would ask someone at Registry to register and log the items. She switched off the lights in her office and went home.

***

The following day, barely five hours later, Dr Nceka was up again, and back at her office. Everything about her demeanour suggested undeterred determination. She was going to get to the bottom of the shenanigans Dr Hans Erasmus was apparently up to before his death, whatever it took.

As promised, Vumile had already delivered a thick brown file, marked 'For your eyes only'. Opening the first page of the file, Dr Nceka saw a black and white picture of a 39-year-old woman. Below the picture, there was a handwritten note saying, 'This is Ms Zoe Morris'. Dr Nceka put the file aside. She would return to it later.

Soon after a brief routine of signing her daily blotter, she called Dimpho and asked her to come in for a quick briefing. Moments later Dimpho dutifully walked in from an adjacent office and said, "Boss remember you said I must cancel all your engagements today. And so I did."

"Yep, that status quo remains. Three things I want though – firstly, that black file on my conference table, it is part of the material I got from Dr Erasmus's house yesterday. I want you to wrap it up and see to it that it is hand-delivered to the head of Missing Persons Directorate at the NPA. Secondly, call the office of the Minister of Intelligence and arrange a special meeting, and emphasise, urgent meeting, as early as tomorrow morning. Thirdly, please arrange a working dinner with the Commissioner of Police, this evening, or whenever he is available as soon as possible.

"Yes, ma'am," Dimpho said, taking notes.

"And another thing Dimps," Dr Nceka said almost absent-mindedly as she picked up the brown file delivered to her office by Mr Vumile Menzeni, the DDG of Special Operations, "please arrange a quiet meeting between Ms Zoe Morris and me by one o'clock this afternoon. Here is her number. I have no idea where she is at the moment. If she's abroad, ask her to cancel everything and be here in twenty-four hours," Dr Nceka said.

"I will do so ma'am," Dimpho said and hurried out of her boss's office.

Enter Zoe Morris

"Honey, come now, be honest with me, have I gained weight?" she asked. She was standing in front of their bedroom mirror, half-naked and slowly checking herself over. At first, it looked like she was doing one of those medical self-checks – feeling her breasts for cancerous lumps and whatnot. And then all of a sudden, as if struck by an unwelcome thought, with her arms akimbo, she twisted this way and that way in front of the mirror, her face contorted in seriousness.

With her hands squeezing the side flesh of her own waist, she turned away from the mirror and asked the question again, "Seriously, Bongani, look at me! I have drooped! I have extra meat on my waist, and my breasts are beginning to sag. Look at them and tell me I'm wrong!"

Bongani, still lying in bed, lazily chuckled as he indeed looked at her shaking her chest and breasts bobbing up and down. She was crazy, he thought, still suppressing his laughter, and then said, with a deep, sleepy baritone, "Zoe, please darling, don't do this to yourself. You're too beautiful for words. In fact, come over here baby doll. Let me do a proper inspection of this problem of yours."

"Oh, so you agree I have a problem!" Zoe exclaimed as she moved away from the mirror to stand next to the bed, closer to Bongani, still feeling her own breasts.

"No, my love, I did not say you have a problem. I said, come over here. Get in here, silly!" Bongani said, opening the sheets invitingly, his face covered with a devilish smile.

"I see what you're doing, Mr Mathafa. You're hedging your bets. *Kanti ke* I still want an honest answer!" she said as she sat down on the bed, with her back facing away from Bongani.

But looking at her back was not what Bongani had in mind! Just as he was getting ready for some more cajoling to get her to turn around, he became momentarily distracted. He had seen her back many times before and was aware of the scars that crisscrossed it, but just at that moment, perhaps because she was complaining about her looks, the scars seemed to be more pronounced than usual. Bongani knew from past experience that talking about how she got these scars was a prohibited subject, which if he dared bring it up now, would spoil the mood for sure, and for good.

So he decided to be coy, "Turn around, *my skattie*, give me the full view."

"So you want to benefit from my misery!" said Zoe, turning around.

About an hour later, the two love birds were still cuddling in bed, and listening to the gentle shimmer of rare winter rain as its drops hit the window pane next to which their bed was situated. And then Zoe's phone rang. It seemed rude, and it gave both of them a bit of a start. It was a private number, and Zoe let it ring for a while, and then with a reluctant sigh, she answered.

"Hello, this is Zoe Morris. Who is this?"

"Hi Ms Morris, this is Dimpho Malindi here. I'm calling you from the office of the Director-General of the State Security Agency, in Pretoria. Do you have a moment?" Dimpho asked officiously.

"From the State Security Agency, you say?" Zoe asked, puzzled.

"Yes ma'am, the DG, Dr Loraine Nceka, would like to see you here at our offices if you don't mind," Dimpho said.

I mind! Zoe thought to herself. But what came out of her mouth was a meek "alright, what time?"

"At 13:00, at the DG's boardroom on the 10th floor of the Musanda Complex in Menlyn. I'll send you the directions," Dimpho said.

Zoe thought for a while before responding and then said, "Alright Dimpho, I'll be there. Thank you."

At just 39 years old, Zoe Morris had seen it all. She was tall, lean, with a smooth, dark and chocolatey skin, and walked in a cat-like manner, like she was a model or something, which of course belied her super-fit body. Everybody knew her as just Zoe. It was only Bongani, her boyfriend of fifteen years, who knew that her full name was Zoleka Anne Morris from Gugulethu in Cape Town.

Zoe arrived at the Musanda Building at just fifteen minutes to one. After a brisk process of being searched and body scanned by security at the entrance, she was guided to a waiting area on the tenth floor, which had plush and comfortable couches. Five minutes later, Dimpho, also tall and slightly fuller than Zoe, her skin lighter in complexion, and her hair braided and hanging loosely over her shoulders, emerged from an inner office.

Smiling broadly, Dimpho politely directed Zoe to Dr Nceka's boardroom, saying, "Welcome Ms Morris, please come this way. Dr Nceka will be you shortly."

Indeed, moments later, Dr Nceka emerged from her office, and cheerfully greeted Zoe, "Ah here we are Ms Morris! Sit, sit. I promise you we're not going to be long."

Zoe did not reply. She was content merely to take everything in. All she did was to mumble a "Thank you, ma'am," and sat down as directed.

"Dimpho, don't just stand there. Ask mam'Mavis to make us some coffee will you. And hold all my calls for the next hour," Dr Nceka said.

Dimpho curtsied rather exaggeratedly as she walked out.

"Now," Dr Nceka continued, just as a stout middle-aged lady in her early fifties walked in carrying a clinkering tray with coffee cutlery, "you must be wondering why I called you here."

"Indeed, ma'am, the thought did cross my mind," Zoe said quietly.

Dr Nceka stood up and went to her desk and picked up a thick lever arch file which Zoe had noticed as the only item lying next to a red landline phone on Dr Nceka's big desk. With the file on her lap, but unopened, Dr Nceka said, "This is all you, Ms Morris, don't look surprised."

Zoe suppressed a chuckle but said nothing. Dr Nceka continued, "Now let's see what we have here," she said, as she started to read from the file, "Your file is rather interesting Ms Morris. You left the country in January of 1980 and went to Angola, where you received your basic military training. You saw some action alongside FAPLA against UNITA in central Huambo. You undertook several clandestine missions into the country, recruiting the youth into MK military camps. You were detained during the state of emergency in 1986. You escaped from custody and ran to Tanzania. There you received initial training in intelligence-gathering. In 1987 you left for East Germany, where you received advanced intelligence training. You came back into the country shortly after political parties were unbanned."

Zoe did not react as Dr Nceka was reading her file. She looked straight ahead, with her eyes bland, but alert. When Dr Nceka was done reading, she looked up and said, "I understand you're now studying for your PhD with the University of Pretoria?"

"Yes, ma'am," Zoe said quietly.

"I see. What I'm about to tell you will require you to deregister. Would you be fine with that?" Dr Nceka said.

"It would depend on the reasons, ma'am," Zoe said noncommittally.

"Very well," Dr Nceka said officiously.

Of course, at the back of her mind, Zoe was wondering what was up. Even though she knew of Dr Nceka, both in her current role as DG of SSA, but also of her stint in the ANC underground. She was aware for example that sometime in 1988 when it became clear that the regime would soon fold and want to negotiate, the ANC had sent Dr Nceka to South Africa to quietly set up the ANC's intelligence-gathering machinery inside the country. Zoe was also aware that Dr Nceka, who masqueraded as an academic at the University of Transkei, had later been withdrawn from the country, just as the exiles were coming in, and sent abroad to train for her current job.

Other than that, Zoe had not had any meaningful interaction with Dr Nceka before, aside from passing encounters at state events. But she had heard of her, in particular her pit-bull-like dedication to duty.

But then it was Dr Nceka reading her file, not the other way around, Zoe thought, bringing herself to paying attention to what Dr Nceka was saying.

"There is a project I'm working on. I need you to do the running for it." Dr Nceka said.

"Do the running ma'am?" Zoe asked.

"There are a number of loose ends. I need you to tie them up for me. Let me explain." Dr Nceka said cryptically. "There have been baffling murders and all sorts of mayhem that is of particular concern to me, which we want you to investigate."

"We, ma'am? Sounds like a police job to me," Zoe asked.

"Well, let's just say your investigation would be part of a bigger project, involving a few other people, none of whom you need to know anything about at present. This mission, if you accept it, is going to take you away from home for a while. It's likely to be intense, and an element of danger cannot be discounted. You do have a right to choose not to accept before I proceed any further," Dr Nceka said.

Zoe thought about this for a while. She did not know Dr Nceka much, but she had heard of her fearsome reputation, which oddly enough she could not detect at the moment. What she knew for sure was that by the sound of it, this was not one of those missions you reject and the assurance that she could was seriously misleading. Certainly, the fact that it was the head of the country's premier intelligence structure that was asking her was pressure enough not to say no. That was beside the sheer curiosity she had about what she was going to be asked to do.

"Alright ma'am, I guess I accept, on blind faith, mind you!" Zoe said.

"Very well then. You are flying to East London this evening," Dr Nceka said.

"I am?" Zoe asked, her eyes popping out. She'd not told Bongani that she'd not be coming back tonight!

"Yes, Ms Morris. This is urgent. Don't worry about Bongani, he'll be strong," Dr Nceka, rather nonchalantly.

"What? What is so urgent?" Zoe asked, losing patience with Dr Nceka, and surprised at her mentioning of Bongani.

"Well, I guess you have a limited right to know. Your file also says you were part of the team the late OR Tambo set up to investigate the mutiny in ANC camps in Angola. You must have been very young then, what, 19? Anyway, enough about that. What I'm asking you to do, besides being completely off the radar, requires someone who has a sense of perspective about the enemy's infiltration of the ANC," Dr Nceka said, her steady eyes looking sharply at Zoe.

"Those are sleeping dogs ma'am. If you don't mind me asking why the interest in cold spoor?" Zoe asked.

"Well, let's just say, in recent days I've come to believe that to understand the baffling present we must go to the mysterious past. You may not know this, but legend has it that American Indians could learn a lot from 'cold spoor' as you put it, about the enemy's future intentions. At present, I'm sitting with a few things that don't make sense to me. For example, in the strictest of confidence, of course, I have discovered a list of the physicists who worked on South Africa's nuclear bomb program. In and of itself there is nothing untoward about it, except that two names on this were initially blocked out. I have since unblocked and discovered who they are. I need to find out everything about the names on this list, especially numbers seven and eight. What I have been able to find out so far is that the two professors are both retired. One lives at a flat in Kenilworth in Cape Town. The other migrated to Australia and now lives in Perth. I'll be getting their addresses soon," Dr Nceka said.

"Will I also be going to Perth ma'am?" Zoe asked, with apprehension in her voice.

"I don't think so at the moment. Of course that all depends on whether there is a need," Dr Nceka said and continued, "I also found a set of numbers in the personal possessions of the recently departed former head of the NIS, Dr Hans Erasmus. Initial investigation shows that these are coordinates of a cemetery in Port Elizabeth. As you can appreciate, I'm sure, when I saw these coordinates, I did some preliminary digging of my own. You see, back in 1989, a few months before Mandela was released, the *Herald* newspaper down in Port Elizabeth reported a crisis at the Zwide Cemetery caused by the sudden disappearance of support staff, especially security guards. A week later, two of these guards were found on the outskirts of New Brighton location, with gunshot wounds in their heads.

These things may or may not be connected. I need to find out what is the significance of this cemetery."

"Oh, wow! Now you have me curious!" Zoe exclaimed.

"There's more," Dr Nceka said and continued, "my investigation is also showing that seemingly someone is targeting apartheid-era operatives. For example, the body of one Captain Tiaan van Schalkwyk was found recently floating in the Vaal River, riddled with bullet holes in the upper body. A few days later there was the discovery of five bodies of middle-aged white men in a disused farm building near the Lohatla Military base in the Northern Cape. Intelligence has confirmed that these were all members of an apartheid-era covert unit of assassins known as 'Ghosts', working on what was termed 'Project Echo'. What they were doing at this location and who killed them is not clear. Even though their existence was known, when the country gained its freedom, they just disappeared into thin air without formally disengaging, and nothing was heard of them since. I need to establish the full facts around this."

"I see," Zoe said reflectively and continued, "anything else, ma'am?"

"There is," Dr Nceka said, continuing, "last week reports were coming out of East London, of a late sixties white woman who was killed by a hail of gunfire. It has been confirmed that this woman was the former NIS head of Special Operations Division – something they called 'SOD'. Her name was Brigadier Elize Theron, and she disappeared in February 1990, almost the same time as the Project Echo gang. Nothing much is known about Project Echo, except that it was regarded as the final solution against the liberation movement. I need you to conclusively prove the existence of Project Echo and the personalities involved in it."

"This is all fascinating ma'am, but," Zoe said, and Dr Nceka cut her off before she could finish the sentence, saying, "Furthermore, and this is a long shot, but I need to retrace the activities of this Dr Erasmus, especially in the period leading to and after the CODESA negotiations. I also need you to find out if at any time now, or in the past, we have ever had an incident of theft of uranium and plutonium, however small the quantities may have been."

Dr Nceka paused and looked at Zoe as if searching for a reaction. But there was none. She continued, saying, "I don't have to tell you how urgent all of this is. In the next 36 hours, we must have an absolutely clear picture of what is happening here. You may not know this, although I doubt it, the President is addressing the National General Council of the ANC in Port Elizabeth in seven days, and we have to make an urgent decision about how safe Port Elizabeth is as the venue for this. Any questions?"

"Well, ma'am, so that we narrow things down a bit, at this cemetery in Port Elizabeth, what will be I looking for exactly?" Zoe asked, with suppressed sarcasm.

"If my theory is right, we're looking for any signs of radiation," Dr Nceka said matter of factly.

"Radiation?!" Zoe asked, horrified.

"Yes. I'll arrange that you get radiation equipment at our office in Port Elizabeth," Dr Nceka said.

Zoe sighed heavily, changed her attentive sitting position on the edge of the couch and pushed herself back, crossed her legs and said, "Well, do you mind if I smoke ma'am?"

"Actually, I do, Ms Morris," Dr Nceka said, with a certain amount of decisiveness in her voice.

"Fine, but level with me, ma'am. Exactly what do you think has gone wrong?" Zoe said, abandoning her attempt to look for a cigarette in her bag.

It was Dr Nceka's turn to sigh heavily as she replied, "Well, exactly isn't a word I'd use for this. Apparently back in the 80s, ANC intelligence got wind of the fact that part of the National

Party's Total Strategy was preparing for what they called 'Day Zero' which was code for loss of power. To prepare for this, they set on a course to cultivate what they called 'friendlies' within the political machinery of the ANC and its allies. These were not what we know as Askaris. Something else entirely. As I said, ANC intelligence did try to investigate this. But I suspect the fog of war, and the excitement at the crowning liberation put paid to all of that."

"Do you know who in the ANC would know about this?" Zoe asked.

"Yep. A former head of counterintelligence at the then National Intelligence Agency. She's retired now and lives in the countryside in the former Transkei. She was known simply as '7'. I have a file on her," Dr Nceka said.

"Alright, ma'am," Zoe said.

"Your mission is to go back to the now-abandoned battlefield. Look for something we may have missed. A piece of ordnance wired to explode later," Dr Nceka said.

"I see. As I said earlier, you know what they say about sleeping dogs ..." Zoe trailed off.

"My dear, there is a difference between a sleeping dog and a dog lying in wait. The former is in a state of bliss and gets annoyed at being woken up. Its anger is innocent and can be placated. The latter, however, is on a prowl, and we have a duty to put it down," Dr Nceka said.

"Now what?" Zoe asked.

"This mission, which you have already accepted, is going to take you away from home for a while, and as I said, it is likely to be intense, and an element of danger cannot be discounted. I'll give you one last chance to reconsider," Dr Nceka said.

"Alright ma'am, as I said earlier, I guess I accept," Zoe said.

"Well, any questions?" Dr Nceka asked.

"Yes, ma'am, just one. Why are you telling me this? The police do have specialised units that can investigate and lead the prosecution of all involved. Why me?" Zoe asked.

"You come highly recommended, Ms Morris," Dr Nceka said, signalling that that's all she would say on the matter.

"OK, again, now what?" Zoe asked.

"This must be absolutely hush-hush. There is a very present risk of society reacting with panic to some of these things. The fewer people know about this investigation, the better for all concerned. You will report only to me, around the clock. Oh, something else I'm forgetting. There is a contraption here that looks like a calculator, but I have been told it's not. I suspect one of the professors on the list I showed you are responsible for making it. Take it with you and find out what it is," Dr Nceka said.

"Ok," Zoe slowly said.

"Very well. I have a meeting with the Minister of Intelligence downstairs. In the meantime, I want you to go through this file. It confirms most of what I have just said to you. Commit everything to memory, and when you're done, leave it here on my table. My secretary will give you your travel information. As I said, you are flying to East London this evening. Or maybe let's make this the morning flight to East London. Further details will be given to you in a folder. I must leave now," Dr Nceka said, as she collected a meeting pack on her desk and dashed out of her office, leaving a mildly bemused Zoe nervously fiddling with a bulky brown file which was marked 'For Your Eyes Only'.

Release the Dogs

Zoe arrived in East London on Monday the 10th of July 2000. She had had very little time to consider everything, much less to sort her own personal life, including abruptly leaving Bongani when they'd already made plans for the whole of winter.

But in the end, it was what it was. As she took the six o'clock in the morning SA Airlink flight from Johannesburg to East London, she was resigned to accepting the disruptive nature of this mission. But about deregistering from her PhD studies, she resolved not to formalise this, and just play for time, figuring that she may still have time to complete it, all things considered.

Zoe did not exactly know what she was looking for in East London, except that as soon as she lands she planned to go straight to the house at number 14 Curtis Road where one Elize Theron was said to have been murdered. What happens when she gets there would be determined by fate and circumstance, she reckoned. She remembered that Dr Nceka had said there would be an element of danger to this mission, albeit undefined. As a precaution, in her luggage, she also included her licensed firearm, a compact Sig Sauer P320, which she had to declare at airports. By agreement with Dr Nceka, for any other piece of ordnance she required she would be supplied as and when such need arise.

The flight to East London was short and mostly quiet because almost everyone on board was asleep. It gave Zoe a moment to think again about the mission she'd accepted. In East London, she would take a long-term car hire. In fact, the arrangement was that she would take the car for thirty days. In her experience cars were a better mode of transport when conducting a largely indeterminate investigation. It was called flexibility of mobility in the trade.

Zoe was a hard person to impress, and she seldom gave a compliment. But she was impressed with Dr Nceka's rather free spirit. In her experience, bureaucrats at the level of Dr Nceka tended to place political considerations above core issues and cared more about being in the good books of their principals than doing what needs to be done regardless of consequences.

In this instance, Dr Nceka, as Zoe figured, was opening a political can of worms. If it came out that the ANC government was investigating apartheid-era crimes, it would be criticised, by powerful voices in many capitals of Europe and America, of being vindictive and of undoing national reconciliation as established by the Truth and Reconciliation Commission, and as set by the example of former President Nelson Mandela. And so for this reason, an investigation of this sort would ordinarily be sanctioned higher up.

But as far as Zoe could see, Dr Nceka was flying solo. Where did that leave her? Zoe asked of her own involvement in this case. She sighed, just as the intercom crackled into life, announcing the commencement of the plane's descent to East London.

Having gone through the arrivals process of collecting her luggage and the rental car at Avis, a Hyundai Gets, which she was comfortable with because it was her second car at home, Zoe was soon on the road. Her plan was to check-in at the Holiday Inn after her assessment of the crime scene at the house in Amalinda.

She had been to East London before, once, and she was with Bongani while attending the annual Buyelekhaya Music Festival. But other than that, she knew little to nothing about the town and had to rely on her phone's navigation app to find the place she was looking for.

It was just after nine o'clock when she arrived at Curtis Road in Amalinda, and soon she located house number 14. The house was deserted, and there were not many people wandering about the street, and no police ribbons were marking the house as a crime scene.

Zoe parked her car near the gate and got out. For a brief moment, she surveyed the scene. There were no skid marks on the road, but the house had bullet holes next to the front door and bedroom windows. The gate was locked with a small padlock. Zoe decided to jump over the fence and went to the front door, which too was locked. She didn't have the keys or means of opening a locked door and was loathed to ask who had. So she decided to kick the door open and entered the house.

It was a mess, with everything a mound of clutter. Furniture in the living room was turned upside down and dislodged from normal positions, which Zoe took to mean there was probably a mad dash to get to the victim. There was blood splatter on the walls, together with more bullet holes.

Zoe took all this scene in, even noting that the bullet holes were not as random – there was a pattern, which could only be made by someone very proficient with guns. Mindful that her presence in this house was illegal, working quickly, she checked under the chairs, tables, inside and behind the fridge, under the bed, inside wardrobes, everywhere where there was a nook or a cranny.

As she was about to give up, figuring that there was nothing to be found at this house, under one of the beds, she found a smartphone and quickly grabbed it. She decided to leave.

Minutes later, on her way to the hotel, she called Dr Nceka.

"Ma'am, I've just been to Theron's house. I need an analysis done on her phone," Zoe said as soon as Dr Nceka picked up.

"Good. Go to your hotel. I'll send somebody from our East London office," Dr Nceka replied, and cut the line.

Within about fifteen minutes of the call, the receptionist called to inform her that a Jonny Martin had arrived and looking for her room number, and she responded by saying they may send him up.

Moments later, there was a quiet knock on her hotel room door. Zoe opened and saw the figure of a young and lean Jonny Martin, who was probably not older than 23 years. With him, he had a rather large metallic silver case, which Zoe guessed contained telephone analysis gadgets of the SSA.

"Hi, is it Mr Martin?" Zoe asked.

"Yes, ma'am, Jonny will do," Jonny replied.

"Fine then, Jonny. I need to know what is in this. Is there anything you can do?" Zoe said, handing Jonny the phone.

"Let's look at it, ma'am," Jonny said and took the phone from Zoe. He put the phone on his palm, as if weighing it, felt its edges, looked at it against the light, and then pried it open. He took out the sim card and inserted it in a machine in the metallic case he was carrying. While the machine's lights were flashing as the machine was reading the sim card, Jonny also took out the phone's motherboard and connected it to the machine as well.

About two minutes later, Jonny's machine made a humming sound, quite like what a printer does when a printing job comes through.

"Well, standby ma'am, it says there're twenty-five pages to print," Jonny said, seemingly keen on breaking the silence that had descended in the room.

"I see!" Zoe replied, with obvious glee.

Moments later, the machine was done printing. Jonny scooped the papers together and handed them to Zoe, saying, "My apologies ma'am, I don't have a stapler. But this should be everything on this phone, at least for the last six months."

"Oh, wow! Including the actual conversations?" Zoe asked.

"Yes, ma'am," Jonny replied.

"Isn't that illegal, though?" Zoe asked.

"Ma'am, maybe it is, maybe it's not. My job was to help you find out what's on the phone. I did," Jonny replied coolly.

"Indeed you did, Jonny. Thanks that'll be all," Zoe said, and Jonny left the room.

Zoe looked at the printouts from Jonny's machine, her mouth pouted as she suppressed a whistling sound. For about thirty minutes, she quietly went through the record of Brigadier Theron's conversations. When she was done, she called Dr Nceka again.

"Ma'am, I've just gone through this cell phone. I'll fax you the printout, but from what I can see, Brigadier Theron was in contact with Dr Erasmus as recently as a week before his death. It seems the two of them were working on a project that has a constant 15 July tag. There is a constant mention of the word 'Echo'. The other repeating number is that Professor Hendricks, again with constant reference to the 15th of July, as well the mention of a remote control. I've also picked up that they have codes. You will see in the printouts, there is somewhat a mantra that they cite to each other before proceeding with their conversation," Zoe said

"Alright Ms Morris, send the printouts. I suggest you go see Professor Hendricks in Cape Town before you start things in Port Elizabeth. He is likely to be difficult but give Professor Hendricks an offer he cannot refuse. I'll send you some of the material in this regard. Leave in the morning. My office will arrange accommodation for you in Cape Town. We can upgrade your car if you want," Dr Nceka said.

"Will do ma'am, and no I'm fine with this car. It blends well," Zoe said. The line went dead, and Zoe set about preparing herself for the long drive from East London to Cape Town the following morning.

Talking to Professor Hendricks

On Tuesday the 11th of July 2000, Zoe arrived at a wet Cape Town at sunset, just after six o'clock. This was her home, and seeing the city skyline in the distance as she was coming in via the N2, including Table Mountain, the University of Cape Town and the three towers of Disa Park at the foot of Table Mountain, fond memories of the place rushed through her head.

But there was no time to visit family and old friends. In fact, barring chance encounters, no one would even know that she was around. She decided to just drive straight to the Waterfront Southern Sun Hotel, where she was booked for a two-day stay.

Even though she'd been driving for the better part of the day, she didn't feel all that tired. But she could do with a hot shower, a change of clothes and a glass or two of wine. She was determined though not to go to bed without doing an initial reconnoitre of Professor Marlon Hendricks's place of abode, which according to a report she received from Dr Nceka, was in the southern suburbs of Cape Town.

About an hour after arriving at the hotel, now feeling refreshed and somewhat energised, with the night beginning to engulf the city, Zoe took her rented car and took the M5 towards Kenilworth. Wearing dark clothes, in fact, a black Nike tracksuit, as well as a provision of snacks in anticipation of a long stakeout, she felt prepared.

Prof Hendricks lived alone in an apartment in Kenilworth, not far from the Kenilworth Racetrack, at a block of flats called Sea View Gardens. Zoe had already received a report that the bugging of the Prof's apartment had been done the previous night. All that she needed to do was make a call to the Prof which she hoped would precipitate a panic reaction.

Zoe arrived at the block of flats, and after a quick and not so kosher negotiation with the block's guards, she parked her car at the basement, and then placed a call to Prof Hendricks. As soon as she heard the professor's haughty voice, she said, "Dogs are marching south. I repeat, dogs are marching south. Come see me in the basement. I'm in the white Hyundai Getz. Now."

Zoe did not wait for a reply. She dropped the line, but not before she could hear Professor Hendricks swearing an unprintable epithet. She hoped this would work as she expected. From the telephone records of Elize Theron, she had picked up that Professor Hendricks, Elize Theron and a few other people are part of a network of people who always say this line to one another before proceeding with their conversations.

She took out her gun, and waited, figuring that if it doesn't work, she will go to the professor's door on the third floor, and take matters from there. Seconds later, however, she saw the doors of the lift directly opposite her swinging open, and a tall figure of Professor Hendricks hesitantly walking out.

Zoe put her hand out, signalling for Professor Hendricks to join her. The Professor slid in on the passenger side of the car, and immediately asked, "Who the hell are you?"

Zoe did not answer immediately. She slowly took out her gun, pointed it at the Professor's stomach area, and then said, "Who am I depends entirely on how you respond to the question I'm going to put to you, Professor."

In her estimation, professors were not trained to react calmly when they see guns, and by constantly poking Professor

Hendricks with the gun, she wanted to induce maximum panic without having to do much physical damage.

"Ok, what do you want?" Professor Hendricks asked nervously.

Zoe took out the contraption which nobody seemed not to know if it was a calculator or a remote control, placed it on Professor Hendricks's lap and asked, "What is this?"

"I don't know," Professor Hendricks said, looking away.

Zoe sighed and said, "Professor Hendricks, I was hoping you would help me so that I don't compel you to help me." As she said this, she took out a gun silencer and slowly screwed it to the gun, and continued, "now, I know you have a problem with your knees. Both of them were recently operated on. I'm going to ask the question again. If you still don't know as you said, I will reverse the progress of your knee operations. I suggest you think carefully before you decide to call my bluff. Now, again, what is this?"

Professor Hendricks remained quiet for a while, and just as Zoe was cocking the gun, he minced and said, "That is a custom-made IED remote controller."

"IED?" Zoe asked.

"Improvised Explosive Device," Professor Hendricks said.

"You made it?" Zoe asked.

"Yes," Professor Hendricks replied.

"Tell me more," Zoe said.

"This is one of two devices I made. I assume you got this from Doc Erasmus. The other one is with Peter," Professor Hendricks said.

"Peter?" Zoe asked.

"Peter Weir. A very dangerous man. He'd kill me if he saw me talking to you," Professor Hendricks said.

"How does this device work?" Zoe asked, ignoring his safety concerns.

"It's a simple wiring operation," Professor Hendricks.

"You mean it is only you that knows how to set it up?" Zoe asked.

"Yes, and no. Whoever wants to use it asks me how to," Professor Hendricks replied.

"Who have you told how to use this in recent times?" Zoe asked.

"Peter Weir," Professor Hendricks replied.

"You have met this Mr Peter Weir?" Zoe asked.

"Yes," Professor Hendricks replied.

"Where? Describe the context," Zoe asked.

"I met him about three weeks ago, at a birthday party in North West," Professor Hendricks.

"Whose birthday party was this?" Zoe asked.

"It was Major General Jan Kloppers's granddaughter," Professor Hendricks said.

"Who else was at this party?" Zoe asked.

"All members of Project Echo, including myself, Aidan, and seventeen other people," Professor Hendricks said.

"I see," Zoe said, and continued "Who is the leader of Project Echo?"

"Major General Kloppers, for strategy, and Lieutenant Colonel Hein Terblanche for operations," Professor Hendricks said.

"Lieutenant Terblanche being Peter Weir, right?" Zoe asked.

"Yes," Professor Hendricks replied.

"Let's come back to this remote control matter. The buttons on this thing are fake. How does it work?" Zoe asked.

"Well, you don't press a button, and it goes boom. That's not how it works. There is a built-in timer which is triggered by specific wiring," Professor Hendricks replied.

"I see. In other words, the only purpose of this is to time the device from a remote position?" Zoe asked.

"Yes," Professor Hendricks said.

"How have you timed the connection you gave to Peter Weir?" Zoe asked.

"Twelve midday, on Saturday the 15th July 2000," Professor Hendricks replied.

"Who gave you that time sequence?" Zoe asked.

"Peter Weir," Professor Hendricks replied.

"Is this reversible?" Zoe asked.

"No, not remotely," Professor Hendricks.

"In other words, if we want you to stop this device from exploding, we would need to have you working on it directly?" Zoe asked.

"Yes," Professor Hendricks said.

"What is this IED which is controlled by this?" Zoe asked.

"Three portable nuclear devices," Professor Hendricks replied.

"Three portable nuclear devices! All of them triggered by one remote device?" Zoe asked, not able to hide her alarm.

"Yes, as long as the devices are all within a fifty-metre radius from each other," Professor Hendricks replied.

"You made all three of these devices?" Zoe asked.

"Yes, me and Aidan," Professor Hendricks replied.

"Professor Aidan van Heerden?" Zoe asked.

"Yes," Professor Hendricks replied.

"How many nuclear devices did you make, besides the three you've mentioned?" Zoe asked.

"None," Professor Hendricks replied.

"The three devices you made; how successfully do you think you were in making them?" Zoe asked.

"Well, we did not have optimal testing conditions, but I'm quite sure that the outcome would have been 100 percent," Professor Hendricks replied.

"But to make a nuclear bomb, you need a combination of two isotopes, namely plutonium-239 and uranium-235. Where did you get these in the amounts needed for the devices?" Zoe asked.

"We stole it in small quantities, at Pelindaba. It was easy actually because we had top security clearance," Professor Hendricks replied.

"You took a big risk, even with your security clearance. You must have had a big motivation. Who did you have supporting you?" Zoe asked.

"The Director-General of NIS, Dr Hans Erasmus," Professor Hendricks replied.

"I see. You were paid for your efforts?" Zoe asked.

"Yes, handsomely," Professor Hendricks replied.

"And that was your only motivation, money I mean?" Zoe asked.

"For me, yes," Professor Hendricks replied.

"Where are the devices now?" Zoe asked.

"I don't know," Professor Hendricks replied.

Zoe looked at him searchingly and then said, "I believe you're telling the truth, Professor. Fine. We're done." Zoe unscrewed the gun silencer and suggested to Professor Hendricks that he could leave.

As Professor Hendricks was slowly making his way towards the lift, gunfire rang out. Before Zoe could get the car started, Professor Hendricks was lying in a pool of blood in front of the lift. He was dead. Zoe had to make a quick getaway, but she was too late. A double-cab Ford Ranger intercepted and blocked her exit, and three white, middle-aged men alighted, with automatic rifles at the ready. Zoe realised that any resistance at this point would likely lead to unnecessary harm. She held her hands up in surrender. One of the men barked an order in Afrikaans, "*Klim uit!*"

Slowly Zoe got out of the car, with her hands up in the air. All three men grabbed her and dragged her to the backseat of their bakkie, and they sped off. Along the way, two of the men proceeded to tie her hands and placed duct tape over her mouth, and then they covered her face with a balaclava.

Moments later, the car came to a stop. With her face covered by the balaclava, Zoe could not see where they'd stopped. But she guessed it was a remote spot, judging by how quiet it was. And then everything seemed to happen very fast. Zoe determined that they were changing cars. As if moving with the speed of lighting, quite like a bag of potatoes, they picked her up from the back seat of the Ford Ranger, and slam-dunked her into the boot of the new car, which she assumed was a sedan, and then they slammed the boot lid shut. She heard the car being cranked into life, and she felt it driving away at breakneck speed.

After about thirty minutes, which to Zoe seemed to be hours, she felt the car entering into a gravel road, and then a few minutes later, the car stopped. A few seconds later, the boot lid was opened, and Zoe felt the rough hands on her face as somebody was removing the balaclava. Her eyes blinked in quick succession as she tried to adjust to the darkness around her. As she tried to shake off a feeling of disorientation, she heard one of the men barking at her in Afrikaans, "*Uit!*"

With her eyes now adjusted to the dark, she could see that this was a farm. There was the smell of animal dung in the air, and she could see a few dispersed farm buildings. As they were herding her to one of these buildings, which she could not make out if this was the main house or not, Zoe tried to scream. But nothing came. Her mouth was dry, and the men were unbothered by her attempts to scream. Clearly, they were in a comfortable space.

When they arrived inside the building, Zoe noticed that there was no furniture, except for a lone bamboo chair in the middle of the room. And just as she wondered if she was going to be tortured, one of the men ordered her to sit down on the chair.

And then with nothing but absolute horror in her eyes, Zoe saw two of the men coming into the room carrying a large wooden coffin. What the hell! Zoe asked herself desperately. She did not have to wonder for long. As if doing something they were thoroughly practised in, Zoe watched as the men lifted her off the chair, and put her inside the large coffin. For the first time in her life, Zoe wished she was fat! Her light body didn't offer any resistance as the men were picking her up.

Realising what was happening, Zoe tried to plead and negotiate, saying, "Please, please! Don't do this. Please! I will not bother you anymore, I promise I will stay as far away as possible from you. Just don't do this, please!"

"*Hou jou bek,* bitch!" one of the men said with a low but hissing voice, which reflected the man's pure evil intent.

"Please, I beg you, don't do this!" Zoe continued to plead.

At this point, a stout potbellied man, who Zoe guessed could be about sixty, walked in. He was wearing khaki pants, a khaki shirt, and rough brown farm boots. Judging by the sudden tenseness in the room, Zoe figured that this must be the boss of this operation.

"Hello, Ms Morris. You see, I know you. My name is Peter Weir," Peter said, a touch boisterously.

"What do you want from me?" Zoe asked, with a steady voice.

"I ask the questions here, darling, and that was my question to you – what do you want from me? Why are you snooping in my things?" Peter asked.

"I don't know what you're talking about," Zoe said.

"Well, it's your funeral. To tell you the truth, I'm not really interested in your views. I'm only interested in keeping you out of my way. I'm off now to Port Elizabeth, to execute our plan, and you're off to six-foot underground. Don't worry sweetheart, we are very nice. See, it is a very big coffin. You will have plenty of oxygen before you die. I'll send your Dr Nceka a message about your whereabouts," Peter said with a touch of finality in his voice.

With growing horror, Zoe observed that the men were not actually violent to her beyond keeping her restrained. She could tell that they only had one objective – an instruction from Peter Weir, to bury her alive – nothing more, nothing less. She decided to feel the strengths of the restraints on her. They had practised this sort of thing back at the MK camps in Angola, and she'd hoped she would never use any of it in real life. Part of this included creating a distraction.

"Mr Weir, will you at least grant me a dying wish?" Zoe asked.

"A dying wish you say? Well, I'm a gentleman. I shall not let it be said that I denied a dying woman her last wish. What is it?" Peter asked, with disdain in his voice.

"Why are you doing this, the nuclear bomb I mean?" Zoe asked.

"Well not that it's any of your business, but it's something me and the Doc have been working on for some time now," Peter said.

"You mean Dr Hans Erasmus?" Zoe asked.

"Yep, it's quite a pity he had to die before seeing his work come to fruition," Peter said.

"What do you hope to achieve?" Zoe asked.

"My dear you surely don't think the war against communism and terrorism ended with the CODESA negotiations now, do you? We are now ready to deal with the ANC once and for all, in one strike. That's what we hope to achieve," Peter said, boisterously.

"And then what? I mean the ANC is bigger than the people who are gathered in Port Elizabeth, surely you know that?" Zoe asked.

"Indeed I know that, just as I know that the strike in Port Elizabeth will cut the head of the snake. We will give the headless snake a new head," Peter said.

"A new head?" Zoe asked.

"We already have our people lined up to take over the ANC and the government. Now, no more questions. I'm done with you," Peter said and signalled to the two men to proceed and place her in the coffin.

What he didn't realise was that in the time Zoe had been asking him questions, she had also been loosening herself. With practised dexterity, which included dislodging her own fingers, Zoe had managed to free herself, and for a while, as Peter talked, she maintained the illusion of still being tied.

As the men were bending forward to close the coffin, their shoulder guns traps also kept pushing forward to within Zoe's easy rich. In one quick and seamless movement, Zoe reached out and grabbed one of the guns, and as soon as her finger was curled around the trigger, she pulled it, with the gun still strapped onto the man's shoulders, and hit his rib cage. As he screamed and fell headfirst into the coffin, Zoe, now with all of the gun in her hands, hit the other man right on his forehead. As he fell near the coffin, dying instantly, Zoe pushed herself out of the coffin.

Peter Weir, who had gone outside when the shooting started, came rushing through the door. He never had time to see what was happening. Zoe shot him, hit him three times centre mass. He died at the doorway.

Not knowing who else was around, Zoe rushed to the sedan in whose boot they had loaded her in. The keys were inside, and she quickly got in and drove out of the farm at high speed. A while later, with the time just a few minutes before midnight, as she entered the city, reasonably satisfied that she had successfully escaped, she called Dr Nceka.

***

"Ma'am, sorry to wake you," Zoe said as soon as Dr Nceka picked up.

"You didn't," Dr Nceka said, interrupting, and continued "what's up?"

"Professor Hendricks is dead, and Mr Peter Weir is dead," Zoe said.

"How did they die?" Dr Nceka asked, coolly.

"Professor Hendricks was shot by Peter Weir's people. I shot Peter Weir and his people. It might be too late to clean the scene at Professor Hendricks's apartment, but I suggest a clean-up team be sent to where Peter and his people are. The place is about thirty kilometres outside Paarl, a farm called *'Die Plaas'.* The police must not know about this," Zoe said.

"I agree. I'll take care of it. Send the coordinates," Dr Nceka said, and continued, "now, what did you learn from Professor Hendricks?"

"He was the manufacturer of that calculator-like device. As we thought, this is a remote control for a nuclear device. It can only arm the device, it doesn't set it off. He made two of them. The other one he made was for Mr Peter Weir. There are three nuclear devices that he and Professor Aidan van Heerden made. They are armed and are set to go off at noon on Saturday the 15th of July 2000. Professor Hendricks didn't know where these devices are. Mr Peter Weir pretty much confirmed all of this, except that he died before I could get him to tell me where the devices are. The late Dr Erasmus was the spearhead of all this. That's all ma'am," Zoe said.

"Very well, Ms Morris. Go to your hotel and get some sleep. I'll put you on an afternoon flight to Port Elizabeth," Dr Nceka said.

It was after midnight when Zoe finally arrived back at Southern Sun Waterfront. After taking a shower and ordering room service, she went to bed. When she woke up, about six hours later, she had a message on her phone notifying her that her flight to Port Elizabeth was scheduled to depart from Cape Town International Airport at 15:30 that afternoon and that both the rental Hyundai Getz and Mr Peter Weir's car would be taken care of through arrangements made by Dr Nceka. She would take an Uber-taxi to the airport.

* * *

On arrival at PE Airport in the afternoon on Wednesday the 12th of July 2000, Zoe was met by Lindiwe Mboneni, the SSA's Eastern Cape Head.

"Welcome to PE ma'am, come this way," Lindiwe said.

Zoe looked her over, figuring that she would not be older than forty years. She looked snazzy in tight-fitting jeans, a beige sweater and high heels. Zoe was not impressed.

"Call me Zoe. I trust you have the equipment I needed?" Zoe asked curtly.

"Yep, it's all in the car," Lindiwe said.

A few seconds later they arrived at where Lindiwe's car was parked. It was a BMW M5.

"Is this standard-issue here?" Zoe asked, looking at the BMW disapprovingly.

"No, this is my personal car," Lindiwe said, sensing the censure in Zoe's tone.

"Still, these kinds of cars are not designed to be inconspicuous. Let's get the stuff I need, and then we change cars. I want a VW Polo, a Hyundai Getz or any other car in that category. If we're going to be working together, I suggest you go park this baby at home, and get something more in line with our work," Zoe said rather snappily.

Lindiwe felt royally chastised! What made matters worse was that she actually outranked Zoe. But she knew that Zoe came with the backing of all her bosses combined.

Sheepishly, Lindiwe opened the boot of the car, while making a call to someone to arrange a group B car for Ms Morris. In the boot of Lindiwe's car, there were white coats, black rubber boots, rubber gloves as well as sonar probes and radiation reading equipment, something called a 'Geiger Counter'.

Zoe took the stuff out of Lindiwe's car, and then said, "How long do you think the car will take to organise?"

"It's already been done. Let's go to the Avis office," Lindiwe said.

"Good, there's no time to waste," Zoe said.

"What are we doing with this anyway?" Lindiwe asked.

"Well, let's go to Zwide Cemetery, I'll explain everything then. Leave your car here. Let's use the rental," Zoe said.

When they arrived at Zwide Cemetery at about half-past five in the afternoon, the sun was still up, but only just. Except for the gate security, the place was largely deserted. Zoe and Lindiwe asked the security guards if they could use their guardhouse to set up their machinery, which the guards duly agreed to do.

With the sun now already set, and darkness slowly encroaching, the two ladies emerged from the guardhouse wearing the white coats that were brought by Lindiwe. Carrying the Geiger Meters in their hands, Zoe and Lindiwe looked rather silly, especially as seen by the two security guards who were observing them with fascination. Two women dressed in white overalls and wandering about graves at sunset was the closest thing they'd seen resembling witchcraft!

The two ladies, seemingly unperturbed by the spectacle they seemed to be causing, approached the first row of graves to take radiation readings. Working on the assumption that normal, natural radiation should not give a reading of more than 2.4

millisieverts, Zoe and Lindiwe were in for the surprise of their lives. As soon as they reached the part of cemetery pinpointed by the coordinates, the Geiger Meter crackled, and its arm hoovered on the red side of the machine, showing a reading level of 7000mSv! Zoe paused in mid-stride and asked, "Did we bring masks?"

"Nope," Lindiwe replied.

"This is bad. I suggest we go back and get them. Ask the security guards to leave. The place is not safe," Zoe said, again naturally assuming leadership of the situation.

With that, the two ladies made a dash out of the cemetery, yelling to the security guards to do the same. In the car, as they headed towards the Summerstrand offices of the SSA, Zoe said, "Let's call the police, and ask them to bring excavation digging equipment. Ask everyone to bring masks. Keep the media out. I don't want the news to break before I'd had a chance to brief Dr Nceka."

* * *

About an hour later, the two ladies were back at the cemetery. Even though this time, every local division of the police had descended on the scene, Ms Zoe Morris was clearly in charge. In particular, she was supervising the digging operation.

Once all the eight boxes that been hidden here were above ground, Zoe asked someone with a crowbar to open them. Having seen the contents of each, she directed that they must not be touched until all safety and security issues had been sorted.

Meanwhile, the police put a dragnet around the cemetery, preventing anyone from even climbing through the fence. Of course, the police, being poorly briefed about the object of the exercise, were joking among themselves about how crime had now reached such heights even the dead were the perpetrators!

At about one o'clock in the morning Zoe decided to call Dr Nceka, "Ma'am I apologise for waking you up so late," Zoe said as soon Dr Nceka picked up.

"Ms Morris, you keep alleging that you've woken me up. Stop it, and tell me what's going on," Dr Nceka said.

"In that case ma'am, let me be straight with you. We're at Zwide Cemetery as we speak. The bombs are here alright, all three of them, and they're ticking. The radiation readings are at Chernobyl levels. It's no wonder the hospitals around here have been reporting an unusually high number of deformed new babies. We're all going to be sick," Zoe said.

"What are your recommendations as to what must be done?" Dr Nceka asked.

"My very strong recommendation, ma'am, is that we shut this cemetery down until the bomb squad have rendered it safe. At the moment, bomb experts on the scene are saying it was risky to even lift the boxes out of the ground, and that risk will increase significantly if we move the bombs out of the cemetery. For now, the police have put the cemetery on lockdown. But it is Saturday tomorrow and there is close to a hundred funerals scheduled to take place here, which we cannot in good conscience allow. We need an Executive Order preventing tomorrow's funerals from taking place," Zoe said.

"That means, even though the time is now half-past one in the morning, I must go speak with the President and cause him to issue an Executive Order that will prevent any funeral from taking place from six o'clock in the morning!" Dr Nceka said, bitterly.

"I wish I had better news ma'am," Zoe said, quietly.

"Alright, I understand. What else?" Dr Nceka asked.

"Well, the second thing I'd suggest is that we call any top nuclear bomb expert we have in the country. If what Professor Hendricks told me is anything to go by, the bombs are already wired to go in under twelve hours. Thirdly, all communities within a twelve-kilometre radius of Zwide Cemetery must be evacuated, at once."

"You're talking about an area that's likely to have over one million people! How and where would one million people be ordered to evacuate their homes at once?" Dr Nceka exclaimed.

"Ma'am, the political questions are not my concern at the moment," Zoe said, clearly unsympathetic.

"I see. Thanks, Ms Morris. Anything else?" Dr Nceka asked.

"Yes, ma'am there are two other things. The five other coffin-sized boxes are filled with gold bars and cash. I've never seen anything like this. I don't know the value of this stuff, but one of my colleagues here says it's probably billions of rands," Zoe said.

"Interesting. And the other thing?" Dr Nceka asked.

"We also found an envelope containing a list of names. This one is right up your alley ma'am. I'll scan it through to you now," Zoe said.

"I see. Thank you, Ms Morris. Standby for further directives," Dr Nceka.

"Will do, ma'am," Zoe said.

Call the President

Dr Nceka was aware that as DG of the SSA, she had the priority attention of the President, and that at any time of the day or night she can call the President and request a meeting. That request would always be accommodated regardless of the President's circumstances. This was written in black and white in her performance contract.

Of course, thus far in her tenure, she had not found a reason for doing this. Besides, she came from a school of thought that said intelligence is about the maintenance of appearance of normalcy even as the storms might be raging beneath the veneer of secrecy. She believed that calling the President outside the scheduled briefing times was a breach of this philosophy and might lead to counterproductive panic or fortuitous abuse of the context by enemies of the state.

But the report from Zoe Morris suggested a response above mere operations was urgently needed. She had to call the President. The time was now just after two o'clock in the morning. In a few hours, the President would be flying to Port Elizabeth to address the National General Council of the ANC sometime in the afternoon. Therefore, the meeting with him had to be within the hour. But first, she had to call the Minister of Intelligence.

"Good morning, Minister, excuse this intrusion into your sleep. Something is up. I'm calling the President in the next two minutes to arrange to meet him at his house. I suggest you come with. It concerns the matter I briefed you about a few days ago," Dr Nceka said as soon as the Minister picked up.

"That big, huh?" the Minister exclaimed.

"It's a crisis, Minister. A few outlandish Executive Orders are needed. I can't say much over the phone," Dr Nceka said.

"Very well, MamCethe, I'll be there in thirty minutes," the Minister said, and dropped the line.

Soon after her brief conversation with the Minister of Intelligence, Dr Nceka called the President, "Mr President, I'm so sorry to disturb you at home, at this ungodly hour. We have a crisis in our hands, which you urgently need to be briefed about. The Minister of Intelligence and I are proposing to come over to your house in the next thirty minutes."

"Really? Can't this wait till the morning? I mean the normal morning, not this witchcraft!" the President asked.

"No Sir, it's quite urgent. Standby, we're coming," Dr Nceka said, aware that she was not allowing the President to dissuade her.

At just about three o'clock in the morning, with early taxis in Pretoria starting to wake up, Dr Nceka and the Minister of Intelligence both arrived at the President's house, named after the late President of the ANC, OR Tambo, and were immediately ushered into the living area. The President, with a cup of coffee in hand, was waiting for them, even though he was still in his pyjamas.

"Ah, I see, everybody is here. Ok folks, now that you have decided to wake up, and to wake me up as well, what's up?" the President asked.

"Mr President, I'll let Dr Nceka do most of the talking," the Minister said.

"So, they all know. That suggests that if the nukes go off and every leader of the ANC is killed, they will be the succeeding survivors!" the President said slowly.

"Exactly, Mr President," Dr Nceka said.

"What is the general background to all of this?" the President asked.

Dr Nceka again cleared her throat and then said, "Well, Mr President, our information is that a week ago an apartheid-era security official was murdered in East London, and the people who did this are former members of a covert outfit which was trained for what was termed 'Project Echo'. This was a sleeper project aimed at engineering one single but devastating strike at the leadership of the ANC. Dr Hans Erasmus was a known adherent of the view that the ANC needed to be brought inside the country and then dealt with. The theft of plutonium and the illegal construction of nuclear devices was to enable this strike. We think that the attack on Brigadier Theron was a clean-up job aimed at ensuring that there is no one alive who can be traced to the nuclear bombs after they'd exploded."

"Good Lord! What is significant about this timing?" the President asked.

"Well as you just said, Mr President, the National General Council of the ANC is already underway in Port Elizabeth, with all delegates already arrived. You, your full cabinet, and the entire leadership of the ANC will be in one place, within the vicinity of the three nuclear devices ticking nearby" Dr Nceka said.

"You say you have confirmed these devices?" the President asked.

"Yes, Mr President," Dr Nceka said.

"Alright guys, you have done your duty. Now I'll do mine. MamCethe, is there any specific thing you want me to do?

"At the moment, two things, Mr President. One, issue a presidential order for an immediate lockdown of Zwide Cemetery so that no one comes closer to the nukes. Two, cancel the ANC NGC until further notice," Dr Nceka said.

"Huh! The ANC conference will be a hard thing to call off!" the President said, with appealing eyes.

"The President is empowered by statute to stop any gathering in the interest of national security, Mr President," The Minister of Intelligence said.

"Not an ANC gathering for God sake! You're asking me to be a dictator to my own organisation!" the President said, with an appealing tone.

"The consequences of not acting far outweigh the feelings of the ANC, Mr President," Dr Nceka coolly.

"Alright, is that all?" the President asked.

"For now, yes Mr President," Dr Nceka said.

"Very well. I'll issue the orders," the President said.

"Thank you, Mr President," both the Minister and Dr Nceka said.

***

After her meeting with the President, with sleep still the furthest thing from her mind, Dr Nceka went back to her office. She had several calls to make, to the police, as well as to units of the SSA on the ground in Port Elizabeth.

Address to the Nation

The time was now four o'clock in the morning of the 15th of July 2000. The President had just concluded a mind-blowing meeting the Minister of Intelligence and his DG, according to whom there were now less than eight hours left before bombs of the apartheid-era were set to detonate.

When the President was done talking to Dr Nceka and the Minister of Intelligence, he took a quick shower, dressed up in his navy black suit, and asked the VIP guards to take him to his office in the Union Buildings. A while later, sitting at his desk and making notes on a notepad to give later to his PA and Chief of Staff, the President also looked at the list which Dr Nceka had given him. He was angry. This was a treasonous betrayal of the people of South Africa, and he would not let it stand unchallenged.

He sighed deeply, and just at that point, Mrs Khuboni, his tea lady walked in. "Ah, there you are Mrs Khuboni, what a godsend! Do you know that I've been up since two o'clock this morning, and I've not had a single piece of food in my mouth? Please, please get me something to eat before I lose my mind, will you?" the President said with alacrity as soon as he saw Mrs Khuboni walking through the door.

"Indeed, Mr President. Give me ten minutes, I'll rustle something up," Mrs Khuboni said, laughing as she left the room.

As Mrs Khuboni was leaving, the President went back to the papers on his desk and decided to call the Secretary-General of the ANC.

"Comrade SG," the President said as soon as the SG picked up, "in the next two hours I will address the nation on a matter of national security. I don't have time for a comprehensive briefing, suffice it to say, we have reason to believe that three nuclear devices have been placed in Port Elizabeth, and all indications are that they are timed to coincide with our NGC which begins in a few hours. Accordingly, Port Elizabeth is going to be put on lockdown. This means, comrade, that in the interest of the safety of our leaders and the ANC as a whole, the NGC must be postponed. As I'm sure you can appreciate, there is no time to discuss this beyond what I'm saying."

"Comrade President, you understand that all delegates have already arrived for the conference! Are you suggesting we send them home just like that?" a shocked SG replied.

"That is exactly what I'm suggesting Comrade SG. The way I see it, I'd rather have them irritated than have them dead! I can call all members of the NEC one by one, but that'll take too long. I'd rather the communication came from you," the President said, appealingly.

"There is another thing Comrade SG. In the same broadcast, I will also be announcing the dismissal of seventeen ministers. Get the ANC machinery together to select replacements. In the meantime, all their portfolios will be consolidated under me. As you know, ministerial authority is delegated, and the President is empowered to recall such delegations and consolidate them for a period not longer than a month. This is exactly what I intend to do," the President said.

"Goodness me! Well, Mr President, as you say, it is your prerogative. Make your announcements. As the ANC, we shall deal with that situation as it arises. I will call the members of the NEC and inform them of your intention to cancel the NGC," The SG said.

After the call to the SG, the President called all his advisers and gave them instructions to quickly draft the orders that needed to be signed concerning the situation in Port Elizabeth, as well as to arrange for the public broadcaster to flight his address to the nation within the next hour. With that done, the President went through the list of 17 people on his desk. He decided to call them, one by one, to tell them that they were dismissed with immediate effect. All of them were unavailable to speak to him. Their phones were all switched off.

He decided to call the Chief of the Defence, General Harold Nkosi, and said, "Chief, I'll brief you fully immediately after my address to the nation. For now, I want you to raise our alert level to DEFCON 1, immediately."

"That's a war level alert, Mr President! Are you sure?" General Nkosi asked, clearly shocked.

"I am very aware of that General," the President said.

"Alright, Mr President, I'll take your word for this. But brief me soonest," General Nkosi said.

"Thank you, Chief," the President said.

* * *

As early as six o'clock in the morning, long before formal proceedings would start, the auditorium of the Nelson Mandela University was already reverberating to the sounds of freedom songs and the toyi-toyi. Delegates from all corners of the country had descended to the coastal city of Port Elizabeth for a five-day policy extravaganza. Even though it was bitterly cold outside, with the howling winds of Port Elizabeth forcing everyone indoors, inside the auditorium the atmosphere was as festive as it was electric.

But then things changed dramatically. Just before seven o'clock, a sombre looking Secretary-General of the ANC slowly made his way to the stage. Everybody was puzzled. There were no scheduled speakers until about ten o'clock when formal proceedings would begin. In fact, as the SG was making his way to the stage, the musician Mandoza had decided to come and entertain the early birds and was about to sing his popular song "*Nkalakatha*".

But it was clear that things had to come to a halt of sorts. The SG took the mic and gruffly said, "Comrades, I apologise for the interruption. There is no better way of saying this, so I'll just come out and say it. Earlier this morning, about thirty minutes ago, the President called me, indicating that he intends to address the nation in the next hour about a matter of extreme national importance, with severe implications for national security. The President did briefly intimate to me what the matter was. I'm of course not at liberty to divulge this. Suffice it to say that after a brief consultation with the officials, we are of the view that the immediate implication of what the President has said is that this National General Council cannot continue."

The SG did not finish this sentence. The whole auditorium erupted into seething howling, with a barrage of a combination of questions and insults being directed at him. His security, reading the hostile mood in the room, quickly took positions around him.

But that was not enough. Chairs, bottled water and all sorts of missiles started flying to the stage. Others panicked, resulting in a stampede as they were making a mad rush for the door, accompanied by the horrifying sounds of breaking limbs as many people were falling or being hit by flying objects.

***

As early as six o'clock in the morning, a few woke journalists started to mutter darkly in social media about earth-shattering events pending in Port Elizabeth. As time went by, the speculation increased, fuelled by the heavy presence of police at a cemetery, and by breaking news that no funerals would be allowed at Zwide Cemetery today. All major television stations started showing a huge gathering of journalists outside the locked gates of Zwide Cemetery, all of them asking questions no one was available to answer.

And then there was more breaking news, that the Secretary-General of the ANC had been rushed to hospital after being attacked by delegates of the ANC at the auditorium of Nelson Mandela University. His condition was unknown, but images soon emerged showing the plenary hall of the NGC in flames.

And then there was more breaking news – the President was about to address the nation on a matter of significant national importance. Television and radio analysts were again on hand to throw their bones in a vain attempt to read the President's mind.

***

At just after seven o'clock, with less than four hours left to detonation, a sombre looking President, speaking from his office at the Union Buildings, with a panoply of flags providing the background behind him, addressed the nation:

Fellow South Africans.

This morning I was informed of a diabolical plot to decimate our project of building a united, non-racial and democratic country, out of the ruins of the sad legacy of apartheid. Back in 1994 when we came into government, we were assured both by the government of Mr FW de Klerk as well as by the

International Atomic Agency that the apartheid-era program of developing nuclear bombs had been dismantled.

We have learned however that a section of the apartheid security establishment, led by the late Dr Han Erasmus, the former Director-General of the National Intelligence Agency, conspired to steal significant amounts of plutonium and uranium from the then nuclear establishment at Pelindaba. Dr Erasmus, with the support of bent nuclear physicists, managed to make, out of these stolen minerals, three improvised explosive devices with enough yield to kill an entire city.

After ten years of being hidden underground in a cemetery in Port Elizabeth, we have today uncovered these bombs. Unfortunately, they are wired to explode at noon today, and cannot be moved from where they are without risking premature detonation.

The timing, of course, is such that they coincide with the National General Council of the ANC, with one inescapable conclusion – to kill the leadership of both the ANC and government, with one strike. Unfortunately, prudence dictates that we postpone this conference instead of exposing this many people to the risk of death and injury.

Our teams are already on the ground trying to manage the situation and to prevent a calamity. There are immediate steps that have to be taken. These include:

I have issued an executive order for the Zwide Cemetery to be closed with immediate effect. I appeal to all who are planning to have funerals there today to make alternative arrangements. I have also ordered the evacuation of everyone within a ten-kilometre radius of Zwide Cemetery. I urge all who are affected by this to overlook their inconvenience and focus on saving their own lives. Therefore, I ask that we comply with this order for all our sakes.

Fellow South Africans, the discovery of these bombs was accompanied by the discovery of two other things. We have taken into our possession quantities of gold and cash from boxes that were buried alongside the bombs. We have not counted any of this yet, but our educated guesses seem to estimate it in billions of rands.

The other disturbing matter we have discovered is a list of some of the members of my government. I have not yet consulted my organisation on this particular matter, and as soon as these consultations have been concluded, I will take the nation into further confidence. What I would like to say in the interim is that the following members of Cabinet have been dismissed with immediate effect:

1. *Deputy President*
2. *Minister of Agriculture*
3. *Minister of Local Government*
4. *Minister of Defence*
5. *Minister of Environment*
6. *Minister of Labour*
7. *Minister of Finance*
8. *Minister of Health*
9. *Minister of National Housing*
10. *Minister of Foreign Affairs*
11. *Minister of Justice*
12. *Minister of Correctional Services*
13. *Minister of Works and Energy*
14. *Minister of Social Development*
15. *Minister of Sports*
16. *Minister of Tourism*
17. *Minister of Land Transformation*

Lastly, I would like to take this opportunity and apologise to the families whose graves of loved ones were abused in this manner.

I thank you

***

It was as if the people had not heard the President! Minutes after his address to the nation, about ten funeral convoys coming from different homes around the city, were seen heading for the cemetery at almost the same time, following the completion of funeral services at homes and churches all over Zwide Township and nearby areas.

The message had simply not filtered through to funeral parlours and to families that the President had issued an order against today's burials. Even the notion of a presidential order was completely foreign to most people, as it had never been done before.

Those who knew, and had heard the President's address, and were still determined to proceed, they were cursing the dictatorial tendencies of this President! How dare he? They fumed. The business of how and when they buried their own loved ones was theirs alone, and nobody, much less someone sitting in the comfort of his office far away in Pretoria, would tell them what to do.

Of course amid all this anger about burials, to some among the angry mourners, the message about nuclear bombs became either lost completely or was seen as a ruse by this government to prevent them from burying their people! Conspiracy theories of all sorts began to circulate. The land of the cemetery had been sold to big businesses in the area, some alleged. They wanted to clear the cemetery so that they can build a shopping mall in its place, others opined. Yet others alleged that the government wanted to force the people to cremate their relatives, something that was going to happen only over their dead bodies!

And so they pushed ahead to the Zwide Cemetery. But of course, there was a problem. The police had cordoned off the entire cemetery, and no one was being let in. The absolute spectacle of people pleading with the police to let them in was too much even for the police to handle. But they were under the strictest instruction not to let anyone in.

Soon there was a traffic jam, starting from the gate of the cemetery, with all the township streets leading to the cemetery, right straight to the R75 highway. In every way you looked at it, this was a mess. The closure of the cemetery had precipitated a crisis of immense cultural proportions, as culture does not allow for bodies to return home unburied. There had never been such a thing as a postponed funeral before anywhere in the greater Port Elizabeth area, and for suggesting this, the President was showing his true colours as an uncultured lackey of white monopoly capital! People fumed.

Yet more convoys of funerals just kept coming and piling up. Matters were made even worse by funeral parlours refusing to take the bodies back to ice without significantly revising their quotes. And no family wanted to pay for any more funeral costs than they had already paid.

It was a truly morbid stalemate, which became significantly compounded by the panic induced by the news that what President had also said was that there are bombs at the cemetery, and were going to explode in the coming midday. Thinking about the coming "hour of the Lord", as the deadline suddenly became known, mourners, especially those who were not direct relatives of the deceased, started to abandon the funeral convoys and joined the mad rush out of the city, not bothering to go back to the house to wash their hands and eat, and leaving the coffins at the gate of the cemetery and along the road, guarded by angry and dejected relatives.

And then there was another piece of breaking news – that the President had declared a DEFCON 1 alert. No one in living memory knew what this meant, and it soon got lost in translation. The poor pronunciation of some of the newsreaders also did not help matters, as the alert seemed to come across as "death come one", which set people's imaginations wild, with some even saying,

"This President is mad straight-straight! He now wants to kill us all one time! *Sizofa kayi one!*"

And if anyone was in doubt about what this "death come one" alert meant, the sight of soldiers deploying in their numbers, driving tanks and other heavy vehicles, convinced many people to make a run for it. The man was mad, and the only safe thing to do against a mad person is to run away, they argued amongst themselves.

Even the ANC delegates who were still recalcitrant about the cancellation of the ANC NGC became horrified at the lengths to which their President was seemingly prepared to go to in his quest to cancel a simple meeting – even placing bombs at cemeteries and deploying the whole army! Some tried singing *'Noma besidubula siyaya, besibopha siyaya, siyaya noma kubi'*, but others counselled caution, saying that by the looks of things, such emotional songs had no impact on this President. The man would even shoot at this venue! And then what? It was better to run and join the exodus out of town. By five minutes to twelve midday, the little Colchester petrol station store and the Nanaga farmstall about sixty kilometres outside Port Elizabeth looked like the actual venue of the ANC NGC.

The Mushroom Cloud

About thirty minutes before zero hours, with all the bomb experts at Zwide Cemetery feeling nervous about the approaching detonation time, it was clear something needed to give, fast. All of a sudden, hardened people, who were not used solving their problems by praying for them, were quietly praying for a miracle.

"We're losing time. Soon we'll be completely out of options. Something must be done, now!" said one of the bomb experts at the cemetery.

He was talking to no one in particular, but Zoe heard him, and asked a rhetorical question, "How much time is left?"

"Thirty minutes, assuming this thing is accurate. Whatever it is that must be done, must be done now," the man said.

"I agree," Zoe said, looking like she had an idea. She fiddled with her own pants pocket looking for her cell phone, and then said, "Wait, let me make this call."

The person she was calling was, of course, Dr Nceka, and she said, as soon as her call was picked up, "Ma'am, I've made a decision. I'm going to load these bombs in a bakkie and drive to the nearest sea water edge. From there I will load the bombs onto a speed boat and drive the boat deep into the ocean."

"And come back how?" Dr Nceka asked, clearly alarmed.

"By the same boat. I know the consequences of what I'm saying, ma'am. We don't have time for this debate. I need you to commandeer a fast boat for me, and place it somewhere near Summerstrand beach, at least I think that's nearest to where I'm. Now ma'am," Zoe said and cut the call.

With her mind clearly made up, Zoe then yelled an instruction to two SSA guys who were just aimlessly wandering near her and ordered them to load the bombs at the back of their own Isuzu bakkie. There was hesitation at first, with murmured protest, but both Zoe's urgent tone of voice and the general nervousness abound about time, a number of police officials rushed forward and gently lifted the bombs onto the back of the SSA Isuzu bakkie.

"Get a rope and tie them tight. This is not going to be a gentle ride, and I don't want these things falling off the road as I drive," Zoe ordered.

With that done and about twenty-five minutes left before detonation, Zoe again yelled, "Folks I'm taking this bomb into the ocean. I need a police escort, as well as manpower to load this onto a boat." Looking at the two nervous SSA agents, she continued, "You two, get in the car with me, now!"

They jumped in, almost involuntarily, and Zoe started the car. Soon she was on the road, and fervently praying that there must be no premature detonation. Along the way, Dr Nceka called and said, "Ms Morris, the boat is ready for you at the pier. The police escorting you are directed to take you there. Good luck, my child."

"Roger that," Zoe said, and cut the call.

As soon as they reached the boat, with only fifteen minutes left, the police again helped Zoe to load and tie the bombs onto the boat. With the bombs tied onto the boat tightly, in order to avoid any accidental drop before she reaches the failsafe line of ten kilometres offshore, Zoe was off, flying over the waves at breakneck speed.

Moments later, with five minutes to spare, Zoe reached the failsafe distance of ten kilometres offshore. Within a minute she untied the bombs and pushed them overboard. They were heavy, and she hoped that there was enough time for them to sink and reach the bottom of the ocean before detonation.

With three minutes left before the multiple explosion of nuclear bombs would occur, Zoe turned the boat around, and with a devilish face of someone about to do the ultimate thing, she pushed the boat throttle forward and pressed the boat speed lever to its maximum. Even though she had taken ten minutes to reach the failsafe line, she now had one minute to reach the safety of the Summerstrand shoreline ...

***

Meanwhile, the news of the heroism of one Zoe Morris, who had taken it upon herself to drive three nuclear bombs out of the community and into the sea, soon became breaking news. All media outlets started recounting her mad rush into the sea and were also showing images of people converging and praying for Zoe's safe return.

But no sooner had the news about Zoe broke, they were soon displaced by more breaking news – the simultaneous detonation of three nuclear bombs, accompanied by images of a sea-based mushroom cloud. Those that had delayed their departure from the city watched with disbelief as the image was playing out in front of their eyes, of a sea looking like it's hollowing out, its water rising and seeming to suspend itself in space, and then splashing down, causing shore-bound tsunamis. Someone prayed for the fish.

EPILOGUE

The time was now six o'clock in the morning, and the sun was beginning to rise. Judging by the absence of any whiff of wind, and the clear skies all over Port Elizabeth, it was going to be a scorcher. John had been talking for twelve straight hours, and the security guards, Ntanjana and Zolile had been thoroughly entertained.

Before they knew it, the time had simply moved in one continuum from seven o'clock in the evening to six o'clock in the morning. They had not slept a wink and were utterly mesmerised by the story the homeless man had just told them. The morning had come before they neither expected nor wanted it to come. Since their drunken stumble into the cemetery's guardhouse, Ntanjana and Zolile had been listening and lapping up every word out of John's mouth. As he ended his story, their bladders were near exploding, as none of them had wanted to take a break while he was talking.

For the first time ever, they became sober, not because they ran out of liquor, but because of the way John told this story. It became clear that even the sound of swallowing would make them miss important plot elements of the story. All the liquor they'd brought with to the guardhouse was still there, largely untouched.

As for John, he looked quite like a priest after a long sermon – sweaty and in desperate need of water. He looked at the two guards with their mouths agape and wondered if they will ever stop asking him to tell them a story. Not that he minded, but their demands had seemed at the time to be bordering on abuse. He hoped that telling them his longest story would make them think twice before they ask again.

He was wrong, of course. Ntanjana and Zolile now looked at him with newfound respect. Their eyes were full of worship as they looked at him, wondering if those who were saying he is mad, were not themselves mad. Looking at John as he finished telling them his story, Jongile could not help but clap his hands, saying, "*Ngekhe! Akukho geza linje.* This man is a genius!"

Ntanjana also chipped in, saying, "*Hayi hayi Hlathi uyinkala-katha mfanakithi!* We must find you a job with that BEE program of Umhlobo Wenene FM!"

"But seriously Bra John, what is your name?" Zolile asked.

John did not reply immediately. He seemed to be searching for words, and after a while, he said:

"The next shift is starting within an hour. We don't have time for a long story. I'll tell you this though – My name is Mfuneko Mazweni. I was born in Bizana, at a village called Nomlacu. I left South Africa in 1983 and joined the ANC in Lusaka, where I received basic military training with uMkhonto we Sizwe. After that, I was sent to Tanzania and then to East Germany for advanced military and intelligence training. Sometime in 1986, I was sent on a mission into the country, together with a unit of four comrades. I was the unit commander. After a series of clandestine activities in the country, I later learned that one of my unit members was collaborating with the enemy. In a fit of rage, I confronted him, and I shot him dead on the spot. Hours later, the enemy, working on a tip-off already given to them by their askari, cornered us just outside Randfontein. Three of my comrades were killed in the shootout that ensued. I was wounded, arrested and taken to Randfontein Police Station. In the police cells, a certain Lieutenant Hein Terblanche, whom I've told you about already, came and interrogated me. After three days of sleep deprivation and torture, I relented and agreed to collaborate, and they recorded and filmed me doing so. Basically what they said to me was that they knew I had executed Comrade Vuli and that they would release that information to the ANC, but alleging that Vuli had found out about my collaboration unless I agreed to go back to the ANC, and grow my political profile for a while. They said they would pay me for this, by making annual deposits to a bank account they would open for me offshore. It seemed strange that they would make this offer. Usually, the enemy uses kompromat, not cash to induce collaborative behaviour. I accepted, partly because I knew that the ANC was heavily infiltrated by enemy agents and that anyone receiving this story might actually be the enemy agent themselves. What Terblanche did not know though was that I had never really been interested in a political career, whether genuine or fake. I wanted to be a soldier, nothing else. He also did not know that I'm generally a very curious person. His offer made me curious about what they were planning, which seemed to be far deep in the long-term. Over time I calculated a persona of madness and offered myself to live life among the homeless, mainly because I wanted Terblanche to regard me as no longer of value, not because I had left, but because I had become sick. I was hoping and praying of course that he would not take the extreme decision about me. That prayer was answered. And so, gentlemen, I became a witness to the events I have just described."

"Amazing!" Ntanjana exclaimed, and continued, "so Chief, you're telling us that you have millions of rands in the bank?"

"Yep, over eleven million rand the last time I checked. It can rot for all I care. I'd rather breathe the Lord's fresh air than use dirty money," Mfuneko said.

"But Chief is any of what you've just told us true?! Because like, hey I'm not sure anymore!" Jongile asked.

Mfuneko looked at both Ntanjana and Zolile and said, "Well, folks, that is how I say it happened."

"Like really?" Jongile asked.

"Joe, you asked me to tell you a story. So I told you a story. Leave me alone!" Mfuneko said, grabbing his daily luggage of blankets, readying himself to leave for his daily scavenging trips around the township.

"But wait man, wait! What happened to General Kloppers?" Ntanjana asked, still hooked on the story.

Mfuneko sighed heavily, and then said,

"Well, as it became clear that Project Echo had failed, that the bombs had exploded safely at sea, a bitterly disappointed Major General Jan Kloppers, who had quietly arrived in Johannesburg from North West, made a dash for the Johannesburg International Airport for a hastily booked trip to Israel. But to his shock, as he was standing in the queue at the departures gate, having just received his boarding pass, a two-person team from the Scorpions intercepted and arrested him. What General Kloppers did not know of course was that since early that morning, even as the bombs were ticking in Port Elizabeth, a team of SSA officials, the police and the Scorpions, using the information gleaned by Zoe Morris from Professor Hendricks, had been tracking his movements. As soon as this arrest was made, the Minister of Police issued an order for the closure of all points of entry in the country, and pictures and posters of the conspirators, including the dismissed Cabinet Ministers, were circulated to the media and placed at all public contact points."

"OK, OK, I promise this is the last question. I need to know, exactly what happened to Zoe Morris in the story?" Ntanjana again asked.

Mfuneko looked at him and swung his luggage over shoulders, and as he moved towards the door, he said:

"Zoe Morris rode the big wave generated by the explosion and plopped with it. Fortunately for her, the bomb itself sank to the bottom of the ocean before it exploded. A big part of its impact was absorbed by the water itself. They found her spread-eagled at the beach, worse for wear, but alive."

THE END

LIST OF CHARACTERS

1. **John (aka Mfuneko Mazweni)**
   (The homeless storyteller)
2. **Dr Hans Erasmus,**
   (DG of NIS)
3. **Brigadier Elize Theron**
   (NIS operative)
4. **Martie Odendaal**
   (Elize's nom de guerre)
5. **Brian van der Bergh**
   (NIS operative)
6. **Tiaan van Schalkwyk**
   (Apartheid Special Ops member)
7. **Peter Weir**
   (Apartheid Special Ops member)
8. **Ntanjana**
   (Security guard)
9. **Jongile**
   (Security guard)
10. **Nceba**
    (Security guard)
11. **Mzubanzi**
    (Security guard
12. **Cynthia**
    (East London resident, wife to Phila)
13. **Phila**
    (East London resident, husband to Cynthia)

14. **Dr Loraine Nceka**
(DG of State Security Agency)

15. **Dimpho Malindi**
(PA to Dr Nceka)

16. **Luca Verster**
(SSA member)

17. **Lindiwe Mboneni**
(SSA member)

18. **Jonny Martin**
(SSA operative)

19. **Vumile Menzeni**
(SSA operative)

20. **Zoe Morris**
(SSA operative)

21. **General Andrew Moss**
(National Police Commissioner)

22. **General Harold Nkosi**
(Chief of Defence)

23. **Minister of Intelligence**
24. **President of South Africa**
25. **Professor Marlon Hendricks**
(Nuclear Physicist)

26. **Professor Aidan van Heerden**
(Nuclear Physicist)

27. **Konrad**
(VIP security)

28. **Mncedisi Mmango**
(List of 17 member)

29. **Marius Kleinfeldt**
(Head of Reserve Bank Security)

30. **Gladys**
(Dr Erasmus's helper)

31. **Monica**
(Hotel receptionist)

32. **Vasily Popov**
(Russian businessman)

33. Abram Sokolov
(Russian businessman)

34. Viktor Ustinov
(Russian businessman)

35. Major General Kloppers
(Retired SADF commander)

36. Lieutenant Colonel Andy Malan
(Retired SADF soldier)

37. Lieutenant Colonel Hein Terblanche
(Retired SADF soldier, aka Peter Weir)